Bottom Line Publications

Presents

Malik's Heartless Mission

D1516285

A Novel By

Eric Lamont Williams

ISBN: 979-8601809344

Edited By: Eric Lamont Williams

Cover By: Iesha Bree "coversmyway.com"

Facebook: Bottom Line Publications LLC

Email: ericw8403@gmail.com

ACKNOWLEDGMENTS

I want to give all glory and praise to God. He truly works miracles in my life and gives me the drive I need to write and give all readers a book worth reading. I would like to say thank you to my family, friends and wonderful Facebook friends who have given me the motivation I've needed to put this book together. Without you all none of this would be possible and I'm very grateful for you all. May my books continue to get in the hands of new readers with the help and appreciated support of you all! As always, I must give a special shout out to my big sister Tajuanda, you know you motivate the hell out of me, Love you Big Sis!

INTRODUCTION

Malik being Malik was doing his nightly routine of selling out of his package and going back to his one and only OG so he could re up with more dope. He rode his bike down Emerson Avenue thinking back to when he didn't have a dime in his pocket and then his OG took him under his wing. He knew he would forever be grateful for his OG and would use his own life to protect his OG's life because that's how real he was. Malik had been under his OG Sharp's wing for every bit of eight months and had already saved up over fourteen thousand dollars. Now hustling was his only focus along with soaking up game from Sharp. Malik was far more equipped in the game than your average sixteen-year-old.

Malik pulled his bike into Sharp's driveway that sat off the thirty seventh hundred block of Butler Avenue. As he walked up the steps all he heard was the normal music and laughter that he always did. He entered the house and seen Sharp sitting there naked in a recliner chair. Multiple women were freaking each other, snorting coke and dancing around the house. Malik was used to seeing this, he knew his OG lived the life of a boss and women loved him. Malik was just waiting for his day because he knew he would be in Sharp's position soon.

"There go my boy right there. My lil nigga that I know is going to run that money up to the ceiling and be better than me. Give this lil nigga a round of applause. He then went from being fronted an eight ball to a nine piece that he's buying on his own now. He did it in no time too, better than most of these sorry ass old niggas running around here. Young nigga in charge and I'm a make sure he goes to the top. Sixteen in high school and still grinding hard, reminds me of myself," said Sharp as he started clapping his hands.

As the women in the room clapped Malik looked at the beautiful ladies with lust in his eyes. He was an outsider in school other than with his close friends. The life of a dope boy is what he loved and longed for. After watching so many nigga's get women because they had money, Malik made his mind up that he had to get money. He knew his time was coming and he was patiently waiting until that time came. Sharp seen the lust in Malik's eyes and laughed to himself remembering when he was a teenager and lusting for older women.

"Sabrina, I think my young soldier ready for some action he still wet behind the ears, get him right baby, take it easy on my lil nigga, don't fuck his brains out like you do mine," Sharp said as he motioned for Malik to go to the back room.

Malik couldn't believe what was about to happen. He braced himself as he watched the woman's thick naked body walk in front of him heading to the room. Sabrina was a thick ass redbone and she was beautiful as hell, her ass jiggled with every step she took. She whispered in his ear that she was about to give him something he would forever remember. They walked into the room and from there it was on. Malik handled his business in that room and lasted longer than anyone thought he would last. He felt like he was on top of the world after his little six minutes. Malik looked back at her like he had really put in work while he put his clothes back on. Sabrina got up and walked naked back into the living room like nothing ever happened. Soon as she got back in the living room she went and started to give Sharp some head while calling him Daddy every time she took his dick out her mouth.

Malik came back in the room to the party, but in a way no one expected. Within seconds Malik had shot Sharp in the head and shot every woman at the party. As they all laid there dead Malik regained his consciousness and wondered what made him do what he just did. His intentions weren't robbery, but he figured he may as well take the dope in the house.

There was kilos of cocaine and heroin, plus pounds of weed and he had to have it. Malik used to black out all the time, but this time he blacked out and killed several people. Though Sharp had looked out for him ever since he had been only six years old and showed him nothing, but love, it was like Malik didn't feel anything after killing him. Sharp even took Malik to his home with his wife and children and gave him a bedroom. Sharp's mansion sat in one of the most secluded areas of Indianapolis and no one in the hood knew where he lived except Malik.

The killings were over with now, the only thing Malik had to do was think about where he would put all the drugs and money he was about to take from Sharp. Malik put duffle bag after duffle bag into the Ford Explorer Sharp had given him. Sharp had given him the Explorer months earlier but told him that he couldn't drive it until he got his license. While loading the SUV he was greeted by guest. A couple of his neighborhood buddies were coming to the house to holler at Sharp. Malik knew he couldn't risk everyone hearing gunshots outside the house, so he used his brain and just plugged his buddies into what was going on. He figured he knew James and Darren his whole life so he could trust them. After all, everyone in the hood was hungry for money. If they didn't like what was going on, he was going to take them in the house and kill them too.

"Man look my niggas I just killed Sharp and some bitches that was in there with him. I'm about to take over the game out here. He wasn't giving you nigga's no money, so I know you fools can't care. I'm a look out for every nigga in the hood that's trying to eat. All I need is some help getting this dope in the car and I'll link up tomorrow with a nice lil lookout. I put that on the G my niggas," said Malik as he stared them right in their eyes.

Neither James nor Darren flinched before agreeing with Malik. They knew Malik was trustworthy, but in their minds, they were wondering how he could kill Sharp. They knew Sharp looked out for him and wouldn't dare give nothing to no one else. Though they thought about those things it didn't stop them from helping Malik carry the multiple duffle bags to the Ford Explorer. They did constantly look at each other like they didn't understand what they were doing though.

Malik went back and forth in the house with a smile on his face that would light up any dark day. He asked James and Darren if they were ready to be the new men on the block coming straight from high school. James and Darren smiled at the thought because their only dream was to have a name on the block just like most youngsters who grew up in the hood. They all made a promise to one another to never tell what happened on this very night. This was the day a new life would begin for them all. A come up was the only thing on their mind's while they searched the living room for more drugs. Malik came back in the house and wasn't worried about any more drugs. After getting back in the house Malik pulled out his gun and gave them both a shot to the head quick with no hesitation. While Malik was outside, he thought to himself that he wanted to be the only one who knew what happened in Sharp's house that night. If he let them live, he was only putting himself at risk for a case or some niggas coming after him and he didn't want neither.

After that Malik headed home bumping his music with money on his mind. He parked the Explorer in his mother's back yard knowing it would be safe until he let things die down. He now had to figure out where he would sell the dope at. He knew not to put the drugs out on the streets too soon because that would blow his cover. What he did to Sharp and the others would be a secret he would die with. No one knew what happened and no one would suspect that he did it and he wanted to keep it that way.

CHAPTER 1

As Malik laid there sound asleep in his prison bed seven years later you would have never thought he committed a crime in his life. He grew up to be quite a remarkable man in the underworld. Every bit of respect Malik had on the streets came from years of him getting money and killing. Even if you were on his side you still had to watch what you did because from experience everyone knew he would change and had a one strike clause. Meaning when you crossed him once you would never have a chance to cross him again. The story of what Malik did to Sharp and the others he killed on the night of his come up never surfaced. Everyone thought it was a paid hit man hired to do the job. Malik ran with the story and lived his life to the fullest. Though by the time he became the man in the streets he didn't care anyway unless it was about the police investigating the murders, his last worry was a nigga doing something to him.

Malik was now a ghetto superstar in the street world, but many would have never thought he grew up a shy little big head boy with nothing. Malik was once so scared to be around others that he asked his mother to sign him up for home school so he wouldn't have to be around other people. His classmates talked bad about him on the down low and he knew it, but just lived with it and never said anything. In his mind he wanted to beat all his classmates up, but the courage in his heart to do it just wasn't there. He started to sell candy in school and created other small hustles to help his mother around the house. He had siblings and felt he was responsible for their wellbeing too even though he was a child himself.

Malik fell asleep and went into a deep dream, he went back to when he killed the man who saved him and showed him everything he knew in the game, Sharp. After Sharp's funeral Malik seen just how much love Sharp really had for him. Sharp's wife Lilian was the only one who knew what to do if Sharp was to ever leave the earth. Lilian informed Malik at just the age of sixteen that Sharp had left him with the plug to any drug he felt he could move. He also left him with plenty cash, cars, and deeds to houses. After Malik heard all the good news from Lilian, he felt bad because he knew he was wrong. He would always find some way to cover up his guilt and persuade himself to thinking he did the right thing though. Sharp had pretty much set him for life if he was to play his cards right and what made the plug so good is that it was Lilian's family, people who could be trusted. Sharp had been plugged with Lilian's family for years. He was married to Lilian for seven years but was plugged with her family for twelve years. Sharp used to tell Malik the history with his plug personally, so he knew what the business was and what to do.

Not long after Sharp's funeral Malik took off in the game. All his years of sitting on the porch and watching the older hustlers had paid off. Malik used something good and bad from each old head he seen. For him to have jumped off the porch so soon he was more knowledgeable in the streets than many who had ran the streets for years. Malik was so mature at a young age that he only dated women over thirty and they loved him. Younger women didn't have what it took to even carry a conversation with him.

By the time Malik was nineteen he was married and before his fifty-year sentence at the age of twenty-three Malik and his wife had three children together. With fifty years to do in Federal Prison he knew he would never be happy with his family again. Malik didn't let his prison time stop him from making money though. While in prison he was making more money than most people made on the streets. He was a man who looked for opportunity in any situation and was going to make the best of it no matter what. His businesses on the streets were still in motion so he really didn't need to do what he did behind bars, but he looked at it like it was something to do. Lilian was left in charge of most of his businesses, but he left things to other people too that she didn't even know existed.

Malik not only made sure his wife and kids were straight, but he also made sure his mother, two sisters, and brother wanted for nothing as well. Malik's mother loved him to death and beyond. He was the only one of her children to never know who his father was, and she knew that bothered Malik. Malik wanted so bad to know his father and was made fun of by other children for not knowing his father. Since his mother knew the pain, he went through she always did everything possible to keep Malik from going into depression. Those behaviors got his mother the top spot in his life. You couldn't tell Malik no wrong about his mother without getting a bullet in your head while in mid-sentence. Malik even told his wife before getting married to never think she could take his mother's place in his life because it wasn't possible.

The crazy thing is that Malik ended up marrying Lilian. The years between the ages of sixteen and nineteen in Malik's life had drawn him and Lilian closer and closer together. Lilian saw Malik go from this short nappy headed little boy to a tall muscular built woman magnet. Though she did used to like Malik she never said anything, she just kept him close knowing her time would come someday. Sometimes she would have fantasies about making love to him even before he was eighteen years old. Her mission was to get him while he was still young so she could mold him into the man she wanted him to be.

One-night Malik went to Lilian's mansion that was left to her by Sharp. He was going to give her money for Sharp's son's birthday. When he entered Lilian's bedroom this time things were a lot different from any of the times before. The lights were dim, music was playing, and she was standing in the middle of the Jacuzzi tub naked. She told him to undress and get in with her. Lilian's beautiful face along with her perfectly defined body made it impossible for Malik to resist. Within seconds Malik was in the Jacuzzi with her having sex that was so good he told her he wanted to marry her right then and there. She rode him in the same Jacuzzi she rode Sharp in for many years. Rode him so good that he fell in love instantly and that was her plan, to make him fall in love. She knew a young nigga couldn't hang with her and she took advantage of it.

Lilian knew Malik was still wet behind the ears and that good sex would make anyone new to the game think they really wanted the person who just fucked their brains out. She told him she would give him six months to see if he still felt the same way. Malik agreed and from that day forward, they were inseparable. The two of them together were a power team and bought whatever they wanted to buy and whenever they wanted to buy it. Malik had never really loved anyone outside of his immediate family, so this love was new for him and he loved the feeling.

On Malik's nineteenth birthday, him and Lilian flew to her hometown in Mexico to get married. They flew every one of their family members and friends to Mexico for their ghetto fabulous six hundred-thousand-dollar wedding. Many thought they were coming to the wedding of movie stars being that every detail of the scenery was extravagant. Their wedding was so nice that a local Mexican news station filmed the whole thing. Lilian thought to herself that Malik was way more thoughtful when it came to a wedding than Sharp. Most of the details in the wedding came from Malik's ideas. If Lilian said one little thing then Malik would put all the details with it and make it happen.

They stayed happily married for only two years before Malik caught the case that sat him behind bars. The best times of his life in prison walls was when he was dreaming about his life at home with his family. Now that he had been in prison for a couple years things were starting to set in on him, but he still wasn't used to the prison life. All Malik did was make money but continuing to do the same things everyday was starting to get the best of him. He was used to living the rich life, but in prison all he could be was ordinary. He was having to take depression medication just to get through his days.

Lilian would drive the kids from Indianapolis to Pine Knot, Kentucky every weekend to see their father. On this weekend things had changed though, Lilian never showed up neither did she show for seven weeks after that. Malik called home to his mother and she hadn't heard from or seen Lilian neither. Then on one Saturday morning he was on the recreation yard working out and they called him over the intercom for a visit. He hurried back to his dorm to put on his fresh khaki suit, his crispy white Air Force One's, and freshen up. When he reached the visiting room, it was Lilian, but she didn't have his kids with her. She didn't look nothing like her normal self, and this made Malik worried. The first thing Malik thought was that someone had done something to one of his children, so he went to sit down fast to see what was up.

"Malik, I'm sorry but I've moved on and I'm really in love. You have been gone for years and I can't live with it anymore. I will always be here for you though," said Lilian before Malik even got a chance to sit down.

After Lilian said what she wanted to say to Malik she got up and walked out the visiting room without even giving him a chance to respond. Malik went crazy in the visiting room and for the first time since he was at Sharp's funeral, he shed tears. Lilian had showed Malik everything he knew about being a man to a woman and now she was gone, he now wanted to die. The visiting room officers restrained Malik and escorted him back to his living quarters. After Malik got back to his dorm he went straight to the phone and called his mother. He was hoping his mother could say something to him that would bring him some peace because his world was crushed.

Malik's mother told him women usually leave men when they go to prison but told him he should be glad because most women leave totally. Lilian was still willing to be in his corner and his mother let him know he should appreciate that. Malik ended up talking to his mother the remaining two hours the phones were to be on that night. After the conversation he had with his mother, he was even more frustrated with himself. He figured he should have just gone to bed instead of calling her because now he was really on edge.

Malik's mother began to tell him about many issues she had went through in life. She even told him about the day her own father tried to rape her while she was pregnant with him. She told him about the days she used to have to prostitute to provide for him and his siblings. She told him she was under the order of a pimp who beat her when she was a prostitute. His mother was only telling him these things because she figured it would let him know that everyone went through things, but a person still needed to keep their head up. She told him that Sharp was the only man having sex with her when she turned up pregnant with him. When she told him the news about Sharp, he nearly lost his mind, he was now lost for words.

She told him about how Sharp would pay her pimp three thousand dollars a week to keep her solely for himself. She told him about how Sharp would make her perform the most humiliating sexual acts on him and record it on tape. She told him about when she came up pregnant Sharp told her if she ever told anyone about him, she would die along with the baby. For that reason alone, she told Malik that she never told him who his father was fearing that Sharp would have them both killed. His mother went on to tell him she knew Sharp would tell him on his own time, so she just left it up to him. Malik's mother was a soldier and knew she raised a strong young man, but she knew he wasn't ready for so much at once. She just wanted him to know that there was always other fish to fry other than Lilian.

As Malik laid down to sleep that night, he could only think about the fact that the man he killed was his own father. He thought about his wife being his old stepmother which felt very weird to him. He thought about his brother being his stepson of all things. His mind was every place, but in his head at the time. At that time, he rolled him up a joint in his prison cell and smoked until he went to sleep. Before he went to sleep, he laughed at the fact that he had killed his own father.

After the way his mother said Sharp treated her, he wished he had of killed him twice. Now he knew why Sharp treated him the way he did.

When he thought about how much they resembled each other he wondered how he never figured it out before. His little brother who was by Lilian was almost a spitting image of him and he never knew he was his brother. Malik felt Sharp looked out for him, but he should have told him that he was his father. Sharp looked out in all the ways that didn't matter and that's probably why he ended up getting killed by the son he really wanted to keep a secret. Malik knew he could never go without telling one of his children that he was their father. Malik was now about to wreck his brain wondering why a father wouldn't want his child to know that he was his father.

CHAPTER 2

The next morning as Malik walked to the prison cafeteria, he was confronted by seven men who were from a ruthless prison gang called Concrete Boyz. In the federal prison system, all Concrete Boyz were known for being scandalous and running in packs. All other regions had to team up making all rival street gangs unite in order to be strong enough to go to war with the Concrete Boyz if need was to ever be. Malik had so much on his mind that he didn't have time for no beef, but he still wasn't a stranger to danger. At this time though he knew if he were to get into it with someone, he would probably kill them because he had so much anger inside.

These guys from the Concrete Boyz were all heroin addicts. They figured they would jump or possibly kill Malik instead of paying him his money for drugs he had fronted them. This is the reason Concrete

Boyz were labeled scandalous and that's because they weren't men of their words. They liked to run debts up and then kill about it instead of paying their debts. The few people Malik did mess with from the Midwest told him not to deal with the Concrete Boyz, but Malik knew he couldn't make money without dealing with them because they all did the drugs he sold.

"A slim you going to have to get your money off the roof from all of us this month, we're not paying you. You never show us any love after we have spent thousands of dollars with you. And we can handle this shit however you want to handle it, but just know we not about to lose no war so choose wisely, slim," said Big Frank looking Malik right in his eyes.

Malik thought to himself that he should have brought his knife out with him, but for the time being he still had to handle his business. Malik might have been a pretty boy to all the women, but he was far from pretty when it came to drama. The guys thought they were going to catch Malik alone and punk him, not knowing he was one of the most dangerous men on the compound. Malik wasn't going to be a bitch ass nigga for nobody whether on the streets or in prison. He just looked at the men with a million and one things running through his mind.

Right when they thought he would be a punk and walk away, Malik hit one of them in the chest so hard that he fell straight to the ground. Malik was always strong even in his younger days when he was just a short little punk in everyone else's eyes. Though the seven men did some damage to Malik they sure knew they were fighting a monster. Each of them was bruised up and the first one he hit not only fell to the ground, but his whole chest plate was broken as well. Malik put him in critical condition from just punching him one time in the chest. It was the talk of the compound because no one had ever seen one man do so much damage while being jumped by seven men.

While Malik's was in prison getting jumped, Lilian was on the streets making sure every drug dealer got their package. After Malik's arrest Lilian was handling all the business when it came to the drugs. Though Malik didn't have any idea, his mother was the woman behind the scenes helping Lilian run things. In his mother's younger years, she was known for putting in her work and not just with selling pussy. His mother was sought after by every drug dealer in the hood before she let a pimp take control of her life. The thing was that before she started being pimped out, she was with a few drug dealers and helped them elevate in the drug game. She could have been the Queen Bee in the streets but figured selling pussy would require less risks.

Lilian handled business when it came to getting money and wouldn't let nothing stop that. Malik's mother made sure Lilian stayed on top of her game. Lilian's only problem was falling weak for men. She wasn't in love with this guy, but she felt the dick was good, so he did have some order over her life. The man was one of Malik's good friends before Malik went to prison. Lilian knew she was wrong for what she was doing but couldn't help herself. She wanted to keep it a secret but knew one day Malik would find out. All about good dick she felt she would run the risk of Malik finding out and sending someone to kill her and his so-called friend. She felt guilty but she wasn't going to let the guilt she felt stop her from getting the dick she wanted. Part of the reason she broke things off with Malik on the short visit she went for was because of her guilt. Lilian felt bad for leaving Malik while he was doing time, but knew it was the best move for her. She cut the visit short because she knew Malik would have fucked her up in the visiting room. The love Malik had for her was outrageous and she knew that, so she knew he wouldn't take it well and would try to kill her.

Malik stayed in the hospital for many months recovering from the fight he got into with the Concrete Boyz. It was surely a battle for him, he did some damage, but some damage was done to him as well. He woke up out of his coma three months later to twelve armed guards around him. The good thing about him waking up from the coma was that his mother, wife, and kids had the option to come visit him in the hospital. Once the guard told him about the option of having a visit, Malik told him that he wanted to see his mother as soon as he could. Malik wasn't only recovering physically from his coma; he was also recovering mentally. While in the coma Malik experienced a strange journey, it was like he wasn't in a coma at all. The experience he experienced was something he couldn't explain so he kept his thoughts to himself.

Every guard in the room with Malik was prejudice. They knew of his street credibility, so they didn't cross him like they did most black men who came through the hospital. Though they did show Malik respect, they also showed him that he wouldn't be treated better than anyone else. He was just another inmate in their eyes at the end of the day. Pine Knot, Kentucky was full of white people who weren't really prejudice against black people, but they didn't trust blacks and kept their distance. As far as they knew all black people were bound to cross you at some point in life, so they figured it was best not to deal with black people.

As Malik watched his mother, Lilian and his children walk through the hospital room door three days later his heart skipped a beat. His mother was all he had and after finding out some things she went through in the past Malik wanted to hug his mother ever since. His memory kicked back in pretty good a few days after waking up from his coma. Lilian and the kids were happy to see Malik. Lilian hadn't seen him since she broke up with him, but they both let that go past and just enjoyed their visit together. They all enjoyed every minute of their visit and didn't want it to end. On this visit they had a lot more contact and time than they did on regular prison visits, they were thankful for that.

While on the visit, Malik's mother talked to him quietly and asked him who put him in the hospital. Malik gave her a few names and was done with it. He was expecting his mother to ask him the question she asked. Only thing going through her mind was tracking down the loved ones of everyone involved and making them feel the pain her son felt. Since all the men involved sent money through their family to Lilian all his mother had to do was get the addresses off the money orders and it was a done deal. She didn't play about her son by a long shot and people were going to see that sooner than later.

After the visit, Malik wished he would have never had it. He was even more down and out after they left. Then seeing his wife looking so beautiful knowing she was seeing someone else only hurt him even more. He thought to himself that it was his karma for the wrong he had done to so many people. Malik was always quiet, but his love for money made him a dangerous man. He was beginning to think that he was better off in prison than on the streets because at least in prison he didn't get the urge to kill people as much as he did on the streets. He still did his fair share of dirt in prison though.

Malik thought about the last time he felt bad for murdering someone. It was a guy who had supposedly stole some drugs from him. Though he never really had any solid proof of the theft, he went off the word of everyone else and killed him anyway. Malik remembered hearing the man beg for his life and remembered hearing the man sound like he was sincere about not stealing from him. However, Malik still killed him. In his heart he knew he was going through the karma he was going through because of situations like that. He ended up finding the dope he thought the man stole months after he killed him. When he found the dope, he went and killed everyone who promised him they seen the man steal his dope.

There was one Registered Nurse by the name of Brandy Middleton who treated Malik like a human being. Over his months of being in the hospital Brandy was the one who put in the most work getting him back to good health. The guards didn't like that she treated Malik with so much respect, but Brandy didn't care and was going to do her job no matter if he was an inmate or not. If there was an angel in Malik's life Brandy would be the one in his eyes. Though Brandy received a lot of dirty looks from the prejudice guards, she still did her job.

Over the months leading up to Malik's release from the hospital he got very close to Brandy. Many would have thought Brandy wanted to be with him or give him a shot, but she just loved her job. Malik did love staring at the beautiful five-foot three model built white lady, but he would never cross the line with her under any circumstance. After all he was a gentleman before anything and wouldn't sexually harass a woman for doing her job. He just appreciated her help.

Brandy came from a rough upbringing herself, so she didn't stand for treating someone wrong because of their situation. She had bounced around from foster home to foster home and eventually started to get into trouble with the law herself. She had a few things on her criminal history, but since she was a juvenile at the time of the charges her record was expunged. That was the only reason she was able to work at the prison. Her husband Doug who was the chief ATF agent of the Southern district of Kentucky, had saved her from a world of hurt. He saw Brandy one day while out to eat and fell in love with her in first site.

Brandy was twenty-three when she met Doug and was with him ever since and was forty-five at the time. She may have been with him a long time, but there were still things she never told him about herself. The reason she didn't tell him these things is because she felt he would look down on her. Brandy knew Doug came from a background where he didn't know anything about a struggle. So, trying to make him feel her pain was a waste of time in her eyes. Since she had no one to vent to she just worked and studied for her college classes day in and day out to keep her mind clear. She was thankful for the life she was living and didn't want to let her past get in the way of it, so she just kept her past out of her mind by staying busy.

Malik was in bed going down memory lane. He remembered the time he surprised his mother, sisters and brother by giving them two houses each. He told them they could do what they wanted to do with them whether they sold them, rented them out, or lived in them. Malik wanted to give them the opportunity to grow in the real estate game like he had grown in it. He was also thinking about the fact that he had never lived for himself in life. Through all his years of living he had never satisfied himself, instead he lived to satisfy others. Malik knew he was sitting in prison because he wanted to uphold an image. The things he had done in life was not in his heart to do. As he thought about that fact, he started to become angry.

He got even more angry thinking about the times his siblings went with their fathers on weekends, but he never had a father to pick him up. Malik had exact memories of everything in his childhood. What stuck in his mind most is how money made him go from being the little lame innocent boy he once was to the man he was now. Money had a hold on Malik's mind because he knew the struggle of not having it and made a vowel to never go without money again. That meant he had to always give the game all he had and that's what he did.

The time for Malik to leave the hospital came quicker than expected. Brandy had nursed him back to health much quicker than anyone expected including herself. Malik's only problem now was going back on the prison yard and not killing someone. He really wasn't sweating the beef with the men who jumped him because he knew his mother was handling that. Once their family members started to come up missing, he knew they would have no idea it was him. If they were to figure out it was him, he didn't care anyway.

CHAPTER 3

Malik got back to the prison yard and everything was assumed to be cool. Malik told the leader of the Concrete Boyz click that he wanted to fight every man who jumped him one on one. He told their leader that the results of the fights didn't matter, he just wanted to fight and be done with it. Two of the guys lived in the same dorm as Malik and he didn't waste no time after the meeting fighting them. The Concrete Boyz couldn't fight at all one on one that's why they ran in packs and carried knives. Malik punished both guys in the room they fought in and met up with the others in days to come on the recreation yard and punished them as well. After he beat all them up the way he did, he made everybody from the Concrete Boyz look like punks. Malik single handedly beat up the main Concrete Boyz everyone else feared. He really had nothing to prove because even when they jumped him, he was still kicking their asses. When it's seven guys on one person of course they will do some damage though.

As Brandy sat at her desk sorting through papers a thought of Malik popped up in her mind. She wondered what the story was behind him. She could tell by Malik's grammar that he wasn't just the average hoodlum off the streets, and that made her want to know his history. She did find him attractive, but she had no intentions of putting her job nor her marriage at risk for him. She just found him interesting and wanted to know more about him.

Brandy attempted to put in the paperwork for Malik's pain medication and was told she couldn't order him anymore medicine. At first, she thought the prison officials were just playing with her but when she seen they were serious she got pissed off and started cussing. She knew Malik needed to be on his medication for at least two more weeks and wasn't going to take no for an answer. She then tried to use all the authority she had to get him more medication. Her whole day of trying to override the denied medication was unsuccessful. She went home that night upset and sad that she couldn't help her patient. Though Malik walked around like everything was okay she knew he still needed his pain medication. His pain medication was the only thing that kept him from feeling pain. She knew that prison officials didn't care about Malik's well-being, but she did.

Once Brandy got home, she asked Doug how prison officials could deny someone medication if they needed it to heal. Doug told her about how prison officials try to hold back on as much money as possible in order to keep more money for their own pockets. However, he did tell her to write up a formal complaint. He explained to her that a paper trail needed to be in place just in case anything happened to the person needing the medication. Doug also let her know that with a paper trail her license would always be protected because she pushed for a remedy before the disaster. He went on to tell her to go to the warden of the prison since they were friends to see if she could get a friendship approval if his medication meant that much to her.

Doug was the type of guy who had no sympathy for anyone so he could have cared less about an inmate not getting their medication. He came from a disciplined household where his parents instilled in him that you could only live in situations that your choices took you to see. Since he was a child his parents always drilled in him to make wise choices. Up to that point in Doug's life he had made plenty of the right choices and didn't plan on stopping.

Brandy wrote out her complaint about the medication and handed it to her friend Jennifer who was the Warden of the prison. Jennifer told Brandy it was approved right then and there. Brandy then called Malik to her office to tell him she had his medication on the way. She knew it would make Malik happy because he had been complaining the whole four days, he had been without his medication. The dorm officer got the call from Brandy and sent Malik on his way to the nurse's office.

As soon as Malik stepped into Brandy's office on this day, she went into a daze. She had been added to two groups on Facebook that she hid from the view of her husband. One of the groups was dedicated to men with beards and the other was dedicated to men in grey sweats. On this specific day Malik had a full silky beard and a pair of grey sweatpants on that Brandy could see a large dick print through. The only thing that came to her mind was that Malik was the best of both worlds when it came to the grey sweats and the beard. Malik stood there for a second before shutting the door and going to take a seat. He had nothing on his mind but getting rid of the pain he was in.

After he sat down Brandy was over there within seconds on her knees wrapping her lips around Malik's eleven inches of manhood. Malik was in a trance from that moment on. It felt so good to him that all he could do was moan in pleasure while at the same time keeping his voice down. He reached over and locked the door as Brandy sucked his manhood like she was a hooker. Malik then told her to get up and undressed her. Though they were in an office, they were treating it like a hotel room at the time as Malik undressed himself as well.

Malik picked Brandy up and turned her upside down holding her by the waist and started to lick all around her clit trying to please her in every way. Brandy was upside down still sucking him dry, they were in a stand up sixty-nine position. Malik was loving the way her pussy tasted and she loved the way his tongue felt. She was also loving the way his beard rubbed against the bottom of her stomach as he sucked her pussy. Her sex life at home had been boring for years so this was the time of her life with Malik. Malik was licking her so good that she got weak and couldn't suck his dick anymore, she just hung there as he licked away. After that Malik laid her on the edge of the desk and gave her every inch of his dick. She gladly let him enter her. After Malik stroked her slow then fast for every bit of twenty-five minutes, he told her to turn over. He made her lay flat on her stomach and humped like a dog until he came inside of her and laid on her small body, still shivering in pleasure. Brandy knew she would never forget this encounter and didn't want him to stop when he stopped.

After getting back dressed Malik and Brandy talked for another hour or so and in that hour, they got to know a lot more about each other. By the time Malik left her office they were in love with one another. They were both missing something inside like a void in their hearts. Brandy would be at home thinking she was happy only because Doug had done so much for her. Malik was sitting in prison thinking about how he had always lived an image and never truly lived himself. It was like they were made for each other because they both needed the same void in their hearts filled.

Over the next few months, Malik and Brandy were getting out of hand. It was like every time you turned around; he was getting called to Brandy's office. No one ever said anything, but people were starting to look like something was odd. Especially being that Malik had been off his medication and back to normal the last couple months. No one said anything, but they were sure looking to see if they could figure out if anything was going on between them.

Malik was so in love that he felt he was fine staying in prison the rest of his life if Brandy was there working. Brandy was so in love herself that she couldn't even have sex with her husband and felt like she was cheating on Malik whenever she kissed her husband. Doug felt something was going on with his wife. He was right but would have never imagined the things that were really going on. Over the years of Doug being with her he knew she had her moments where she didn't want to be bothered by no one, not even him. He never knew what made her that way, but he would give her the space she wanted when those times came around. This time it felt different to him, so he kept a close eye on her.

Lilian came across Malik's mind at times, but she was the last person he stressed about after he fell in love with Brandy. Life was great for Malik and he refused to let anyone steal the peace of mind he now had. Even when guards got smart with him, he didn't even reply. He wasn't going to let anything get in the way of his love life with Brandy. Over the few months him and Brandy were together they told each other their every thought. Brandy had finally got to hear Malik's story as she had wanted to from the start. After hearing about him always wanting to know his father and about the way his wife did him, she started to feel compassion for him. Malik didn't tell Brandy the full story about his father, but he told her enough. Brandy found herself trying to find Malik's father for him, but it was not successful at all for her.

Brandy had just left work and Malik was on his way back to his housing unit when he heard his name over the intercom. He was told to go see his case manager, since he was already headed to the dorm, he just brushed it off. Once he got to the dorm he almost passed out when he heard he would be put in to transfer prisons the following morning. Malik tried to deny the transfer but was told he couldn't deny this type of transfer. His case manager informed him that his points had dropped down to medium security points from high security. There was no way he could sit in a high security prison with medium points because the prison would be at fault if something was to happen to him. The case manager explained to Malik that the prison point system was made by prison officials and he had no say so on where anyone was housed. Malik got up and cussed out his case manager, afterwards he went to his cell. He didn't even have enough will power to get in the shower after the news he was told.

Malik felt the world was crashing in on him. His mind was so messed up that he was thinking about committing suicide. He had gotten so close to Brandy that he felt he wouldn't be able to live without her. His feelings for her were so deep that he had gotten her name tattooed on him. When he got her name tattooed on him, he knew he was taking a big risk of prison officials finding out about their relationship, but he didn't care. Malik's infatuation to Brandy was scary if you were looking in from the outside. At the same time Brandy felt the same way about him and this was in no way normal. He eventually took some high dosage sleeping medication and went to sleep.

Lilian was at home snorting a line of cocaine when she started to think about Malik. She had been with other men, but she was still lonely without her husband. As she snorted her line, she thought about how Malik used to make fun of her when she snorted. Though he didn't snort himself he never looked down on anybody who did. He knew Lilian snorted before he married her, so he couldn't get mad, but he did tell her how funny it looked. She would always tell him to try it or shut up and they would both laugh about it.

Lilian thought about the fact that Malik hadn't called her in a few months. She wanted to take his kids to see him. His son's birthday was coming up so she figured she would take him to see his dad. Lilian knew the visit would make Malik's day as well as his son's. Malik was still the love of Lilian's life, but she knew she didn't have it in her to wait for his fifty-year prison term to be over with. She wanted to enjoy life and knew she wasn't promised to even be living in fifty years. Lilian had told Malik to quit serving his friend Montario. She told him that Montario didn't seem like he was about the right and like he had weakness in his blood. Malik told her she was tripping and to stay out of his business. After a two-year investigation on Malik for drugs and several failed attempts to arrest him the police caught a break when they pulled Montario over one night. He told them he had information on Malik. From then on Montario did many controlled buys with Malik until police built up enough evidence to arrest him. In his trial the man Lilian told him to leave alone numerous times was the one who testified and got him fifty years in prison. In the end Malik could only be mad at himself because he was the one who never wanted to listen to anybody.

Brandy came into work with Malik on her mind. She called him to her office for his morning observation which they only used to have sex. On this day Malik went into Brandy's office with the saddest look on his face. He held in every tear until he got in her office and shut the door. Brandy ran to his side asking him what was wrong with him. He then told her about him being put in for a transfer. That's when she broke out in tears and he did the same. This was the last thing Brandy was expecting or wanted to hear. They hugged the whole visit not even letting go of each other to have their normal morning sex.

The following day when Malik was called to Brandy's office, he took his time to get there. He was trying to figure out how he would carry on in a new prison without Brandy. When he got to her office they kissed and tried to figure out how he could stay in the prison. Though all the ways sounded good to the ear on keeping him there they both knew it wouldn't happen. Brandy knew she could at least hold off the transfer by putting a medical hold on him, but medical holds didn't last forever so she was still thinking of other ways to keep him with her.

After weeks of not coming up with a plan to keep Malik in the prison, they started planning to live without one another. Brandy told him that she would get a transfer to whatever prison they sent him to. Malik wasn't too sure about that happening, but it was the only hope he had so he just ran with it. They still had thirty more days left on the medical hold so they just hoped something would come up and they would be able to continue being with each other.

Three weeks later Lilian was at the prison with the kids to see Malik. Lilian was used to waiting in the visiting room a little while for Malik. This time she was waiting two hours before the guards walked up to her table and told her Malik refused the visit. After that Lilian had what looked like a nervous breakdown in the visiting room. His kids began to cry because they wanted to see their dad. Lilian now felt hurt like she never had before. She couldn't believe the man she truly loved was refusing to see her. She knew he had to have known his children were with her and knew he knew it was his son's birthday. Him refusing the visit let her know that Malik must have hated her. The feeling of him hating her brought the feeling of emptiness to her heart. Lilian's life was over now from her point of view. She never thought in a million years she would hurt him to the extent that he would refuse a visit with her especially since he was the one locked up.

Malik sat in his prison cell feeling in his heart he did the right thing by refusing his visit with Lilian and his children. He felt he would have been cheating on Brandy if he had of went out on the visit. Plus, he had mixed emotions about Lilian. One minute he wanted to let her live her life and the next he wanted to send his trained killers out to kill her, since she played him. Though he was in prison he could still have her killed and Lilian knew this off top. He knew for sure he had no desire at all to be with Lilian. Brandy was the only woman he wanted to make happy and she was the only woman who made him happy.

Brandy got so desperate trying to find a way to keep Malik in the prison that she went to the warden to see if she could keep Malik at the prison. The warden told her that she would see if she could override the transfer. She also told Brandy she couldn't promise she could get central office to let him stay. What Brandy didn't know is that the warden had a crush on Malik too. While Malik was in the hole for a fight, he had a chance to get up close and personal with the warden and the sex he gave her was still on her mind. She knew she would have her chance again one day if he stayed, so she planned to put in her best effort to keep him there. The warden and Brandy were good friends, but she wasn't helping because of their friendship. She was helping because she wanted some more dick from Malik.

The only true friend Malik had in the prison was set to go home in a few weeks, so Malik was dealing with a lot. His friend Reggie was the only one he talked to that gave him back advice he could feel. Malik was sad his friend was going home, but happy for him at the same time. Reggie had been down for over thirty years and was well due for his release date. Reggie was the only one who knew about Malik's relationship with Brandy. Malik never told anyone else about his love affair with Brandy. Reggie told Malik how to smuggle his knives into the next prison he was going to. He also explained to Malik that lower security prison was way better than high security. Reggie didn't know that

Malik wanted to stay in high security so he could be with Brandy. Malik didn't care about the danger of a high security prison or none of that, he just wanted to be with Brandy. Many men sat in high security prison praying to go to lower security, but not Malik because he knew he was going to remain a man no matter what prison he was in.

The next day the medical hold on Malik was taken off him, but the warden put him on a mental health evaluation hold to hold him longer. Reggie told Malik the best thing for him to do was leave the prison. Reggie told him that because he knew when he was released from prison the Concrete Boyz would kill Malik. Reggie was the only one stopping the Concrete Boyz from killing him. Malik didn't care what Reggie was talking about he already had his mind made up that he wanted to stay at the same prison he was at. Malik didn't give a damn about the Concrete Boyz or no one else.

Malik was caught up in a tight situation, but he had never been a quitter. He was a determined individual who always figured a way out of no way. He thought about everything Reggie had said, but Reggie didn't know that Malik was in love. Malik even got on his knees and asked in prayer for the transfer to be lifted off him. He knew he could get another woman in a different prison, but he only wanted Brandy.

CHAPTER 4

It took about two weeks before Malik learned that there was no way for him to stay at the prison with the love of his life. In those two weeks he had started going to church for the first time since his childhood and praying every night. His reason for going to church was because he needed help with soothing his mind of everything going on in his life. He felt like the preacher was talking about his life every time he preached. Malik was starting to feel like God was trying to tell him something. For the first time since he heard about his transfer Malik was starting to feel whole again. He was happy to call home every night and talk to his mother about different scriptures in the Bible. Though he was still broken, he was starting to see light at the end of the tunnel.

Now that Malik was starting to get some stableness to his mind, he started back running on the track and lifting weights. Brandy gave him full body massages every time he went to her office. They knew they were going to miss each other, but they still had hope that somehow, they would remain together. Brandy told Malik from the beginning she would transfer to whatever prison he went to and now that was the only hope Malik had. They figured she should wait a few months then put in for the transfer. She planned to divorce her husband beforehand. Brandy had no desire for Doug anymore in no type of way, she got irritated when he even touched her. She quit having sex with Doug after the first time she had sex with Malik. In her mind she figured her husband might have been doing something on the side too, considering he never asked for sex or complained about not having any.

Over the weeks of Malik's pending transfer, him and Brandy had sex so much that he was getting tired of it. She gave him head in every position and they had used every sex position. He busted so many nuts in her one day that he had to rebuild his sperm count before anything would come out when he busted a nut. They were just preparing for the few months they would be without each other. This in no way was going to be an easy departure for either of them. They knew it had to happen though, so they just prepared for the departure. They also looked at the good fact that Malik would be going to a much safer prison.

Malik was preparing to file his appeal on his federal sentence. Though he was pretty much caught dead wood, he still had a good chance of the appeal going in his favor. He had the best lawyer in Indianapolis representing him on his federal charges. Yes, his friend did testify on him, but his lawyer had found multiple loopholes in Montario's testimony. One reason was because Montario had previously testified on four men in a murder trial and was caught in lies. All four men were sentenced to life in prison, but their terms were overturned due to the lies Montario told.

Also because of Montario's mental health history, he was known to have theories that no one else knew about. Montario was known for telling people things they did that never happened. Malik told Brandy of his lawyer's new findings and she was overwhelmed with joy. She prayed that Malik would be released before she could even transfer to his new prison. She couldn't help but to get down and suck his dick after he told her the good news.

Reggie was due to go home the next morning so Malik threw him the best prison party an inmate could ask for, even though Reggie didn't stay out for the party. Instead Reggie was in the room looking over Malik's paperwork seeing if he really had a chance of winning his appeal. To Malik's surprise Reggie told him that he would win his appeal for sure. Reggie explained to him that after a lawyer finds true grounds to discredit a testimony the time is always overturned. Especially since the witness's testimony was the only evidence the prosecutors had against him. He told Malik that he would see him on the streets and that's when they would really party. Reggie and Malik sat back and talked all the way until it was time to lockdown. In prison it was hard seeing your partners go home, but you would still be happy for them. Reggie and Malik shook hands at lockdown time then went to their separate cells. They both knew they would miss each other dearly.

Brandy laid in bed next to her husband on this night and the only person on her mind was Malik. She knew he would be transferred that week and was just preparing for life without him. Since his appeal was to be granted soon, she knew it wouldn't be long before he was home. She was now thinking about how she would break things off with her husband. She knew it wouldn't be easy for Doug because he had changed his whole life just to be with her. She was tired of being unhappy with Doug though. She wanted Doug out of her life and that was the bottom line. Her new man was Malik and she didn't care about the distance or the situation she was going to remain faithful to him.

While the rest of the prison compound was still sleep officers were up doing three releases. Officers unlocked Reggie's cell to start his release process. Malik heard Reggie's cell door unlock and jumped to his feet and went to the cell window. The only thing you could see was eyeballs staring out of Malik's cell window, he always kept his room dark. Reggie couldn't even look Malik's direction because he didn't know what would happen to Malik from that point forward. Malik knew that Reggie had his back and would do anything he could to help him. He was grateful for Reggie for a lot of reasons.

"Reggie Robinson if you want to go home get your black ass up here now," said the officer while unlocking Reggie's cell from the control panel and talking into the intercom.

Within five seconds Reggie was at the officer's desk saying, "yessir I'm here and ready to go."

The officer laughed at the way Reggie said "yessir" and was also laughing because he was at the desk right after his door unlocked. Officer Bryant had been there watching over Reggie for the last twenty-two years. He laughed at giving his buddy a hard time before releasing him to go home. They sat at the desk and did some of Reggie's release paperwork. After that they shook hands then he was off to the warden's office to complete the final step of his release process. After that he was going to be a free man or at least he thought he was going to be a free man. He had been locked up for so long that he didn't know if he should feel happy or sad.

After the warden fingerprinted him, he walked out the door to breathe the air of freedom. He told the newfound love of his life he wanted her to pick him up in an SUV and that's what she did. She pulled the white Ford Expedition up to the end of the walkway to pick him up and take him away from the prison. Not even a second after he sat on the seat of the SUV it was gone in the wind. Prison days were over for him and in his mind, he knew he would rather die than to go back to prison. He told her to take him straight to Taco Bell and that's where they went before jumping on the highway and heading to a peaceful place.

Back at the prison it was count time. Malik's cellmate got up for count and tried to wake Malik up for count like he did every day that Malik tried to sleep through count. His cellmate never wanted him to get a disciplinary write up for refusing count, so he always woke him up. The officers got to the door and told Malik's cell mate to get him to move, but Malik wouldn't move. The officers then went into his cell, but they couldn't get him to move neither. They checked his pulse after that and though he had one he was still barely breathing. The officers called medical and rushed him to the hospital section of the prison. They called Brandy on the phone, but she hadn't got to work yet. Since Brandy hadn't made it to work yet the officers were going to have to send Malik to an outside hospital for treatment. No one else in the medical department had the credentials Brandy had so they couldn't treat Malik.

The escort officer finally surfaced to take Malik to the hospital but stopped when he seen what he seen. It wasn't Malik laying there on the bed, it was Reggie Robinson. The officer immediately called for the prison to be locked down. He had no knowledge of Reggie going home and no idea of what was going on. The officers who were there were rookies who didn't know the inmates like the officers who had been there a while did. The escort officer knew both Malik and Reggie very well, he knew it was Reggie in Malik's bed. After going to Reggie's cell and seeing he had been released the escort officer knew Malik had escaped. He then knew that everyone who worked in the prison was about to have a lot of work on their hands.

After the prison was locked down an FBI team was called into the prison. They wondered how an inmate could get past the finger printing system and the warden. The head FBI investigator called the warden into a private room to question her on more than one topic. No one knew the warden took medication every night that made her drowsy for multiple hours upon her waking up. She never came into work before ten in the morning because she had to give her medication enough time to wear off from taking it the night before. On this morning she came into work early because her assistant told her he was taking the day off. Then the FBI investigator wondered how an inmate could have passed the fingerprint verification. The warden was put on administrative leave so the FBI could do their investigation. They didn't believe the warden's story though it did sound good. From that point on their mission was to find charges to file on her for recklessly releasing a dangerous inmate from prison.

Three hours had passed before everyone noticed Brandy didn't show up for work. They called her house and got an answer from her husband. The FBI and prison officials informed him that his wife never came in for work that morning. Doug threw the phone, grabbed his shotgun and headed in the path his wife took to work every day. His search came up empty and then he headed to the prison. Once Doug entered the prison, he was told by prison officials that they believed she helped an inmate escape. That's when Doug asked if the inmates name was Malik, when he was told yes, he stormed out the prison. Doug went to his truck and started beating on the steering wheel with his bare fist until they started to bleed. He couldn't believe his wife had left him and their children. This was something he couldn't sleep on; he planned to stay up until he found his wife.

Malik was in the Expedition still amazed that the plan him and Brandy put together worked. They had been putting the plan together for two long months. Brandy had to sacrifice a lot, but she felt it was worth the sacrifice. Malik's mind was so in a maze that he couldn't even talk, all he could do was shake his head listening to the music. He couldn't believe Brandy really did what she did for him. After all he was in love, but he had never in life had no one take such a risk for him and on top of that leave a family behind. That only made Malik love Brandy even more.

Brandy and Malik had a rock-solid plan to get him out of prison but didn't have such a solid plan for after his escape. Brandy had a duck off spot for them in

Tennessee, but knew they would be pushing for time, so she told Malik to put on his thinking cap. They pulled over to what looked like the middle of nowhere and switched cars. This was their fourth time switching cars. Brandy had done her planning well and had six cars ducked off for them to switch vehicles frequently on the way to Tennessee.

Brandy told Malik she felt Tennessee was the best place for them to go at the time because the cops were going to be heavy on the highway. She knew they would be looking in surrounding states. She also knew they would be looking for long distance traveling too. She figured the place she had picked out for them was the last place anyone would look for them. It was a cabin in an isolated area where no one had been for years. She knew no one had been there because the ribbon she left in the door seventeen years earlier fell to the ground when she opened the door. She knew if someone had been inside it would have already been on the floor. She stumbled up on the place years before Malik's escape. She was out with friends on a girl's trip when they got lost and found the place. They partied in the cabin like it was theirs before the left.

The weather was warm on this spring day. The cabin they were in was nicely decorated with a Jacuzzi tub and a walk-in shower. They didn't waste any time before they were all over each other. They made a fire in the fireplace and made love in front of it for the first time outside of prison. This time Brandy could let out her moans and not have to be worried about another officer hearing her. She rode Malik until he came inside of her.

After making love they held each other and talked. Brandy told Malik she was having a baby. That made Malik mad because they were now on the run. He told her she should have told him before he escaped. He told her he would have just waited on his appeal if he had of known a baby was in the picture. Now they were in a serious situation, though Malik didn't stress, after all he knew Brandy was a Registered Nurse. Malik knew they could figure out how to deliver and take care of a baby if they did the impossible by plotting a successful escape from federal prison. They made love again before they went to bed. Malik held her close to his body and wouldn't let her go.

Back at the prison investigators were still trying to figure out how someone was able to escape from federal custody. The whole story sounded weird to all the investigators. The warden was in the clear because she had it in her paperwork that she took medication. Investigators were mad at the warden because they felt she should have had someone else doing releases if she knew her medication made her so drowsy that she would release the wrong inmate. The releasing officer followed protocol so no one could hold him at fault. The investigators kept it simple by saying they were just outsmarted. In no way was this escape a good sign for the prison system.

The doctors told Reggie that he had passed out from an overdose of heroin. Reggie looked at the doctor and told him he was a liar. The doctor then showed him the charts and Reggie told the doctor he had to have been drugged. Once officers found out what had happened to Reggie, they automatically concluded that Malik had drugged him. Now that they knew Reggie was in the clear they had to release him from prison, which both Reggie and Malik knew would happen from the start. The evidence didn't point to Reggie being involved so investigators had no choice but to release him.

What investigators didn't know is that the escape was plotted out and every detail about the escape was thought out very carefully. The warden and Brandy were good friends, so the warden didn't hesitate to assist Brandy when she came to her with the bullet proof plan. Plus, Brandy gave the warden one hundred thousand dollars cash for the favor. The releasing officer was paid off as well. Reggie had talked to the officer before time and he agreed to let the release go through as long as he was paid. After that they were stuck with trying to figure out how to get past the fingerprinting system. That's when the warden told Malik to not actually touch the machine but instead hold his finger right above the scanner. Once Malik held his finger above the scanner the warden manually accepted the fingerprint. Doing it this way no one would be able to say she let Malik past without fingerprinting him. Only thing the investigators could do was sit there and be stuck in their own thoughts. Doug knew his wife had it in her to figure some things out, but he didn't know she could think out a plan to escape federal prison. The warden also wanted to have sex with Malik again after his escape from prison. If it wasn't for Brandy promising her Malik would have sex with her, she wouldn't have agreed to let him escape.

Doug sat in his seat that night just wondering where his wife was at. He thought about every place she could be but couldn't figure out where she might have run off to. Doug hated that his wife was now fucking a black man. He knew he was in for the task of his lifetime, but it was about his wife and he had no plans to give up on finding her.

CHAPTER 5

The next morning Brandy woke Malik up to breakfast in bed. She told him they needed to talk about what they would do to make money from that point forward. Malik told her that he had money they could go to Indianapolis and pick up. Brandy shot the idea down right from the beginning. She thought to herself that Malik should have known to be much smarter than that. Going back to his hometown would have been more like turning himself into the police. Malik was determined to go back but did change his mind after she explained every point to him. He then asked her what they would do because his plan was to go pick up money he already had. He told her he would have had extra money sent other than the money to pay off the warden and the release officer if he had of known she didn't want to go back to Indianapolis.

After talking they sat there and ate in silence, both with many thoughts on their minds. Brandy asked Malik if he had ever thought about the true value he had. Malik looked at her and told her he had always lived up to his fullest potential. Then went on to tell her that he had more money than the President. She smiled at him and asked him to be quiet for a second and listen. He sat there and smiled because a woman had never told him anything like that, but he liked it because now he wasn't the only one having to think.

Brandy told him that he was a lady's magnet and if he got on Plenty of Fish or Tinder, he would be able to find rich women and use them for their money. Malik looked at her and asked her what Plenty of Fish and Tinder even was. She then told him they were dating sites where women pretty much gave themselves to men who spoke the right words to them. He sat there and thought for a few minutes and then told her he was down for the cause. She told him it was a bold move so once he met the women, they would have to move fast with him getting money out of them. She knew this could happen if things were planned out just right. It was all about when her and Malik's pictures would be aired on TV, which she knew would be soon.

Malik looked at Brandy and thought to himself about how much of a soldier she was. He didn't know he could ever meet a woman about her hustle as much as him. For her to tell him she would let him go on dates with other women for money only meant her mind was about money and that's what Malik needed. Malik thought to himself about when girls in school used to make fun of him and his big sister would have to fight for him. He was happy that Brandy found him so attractive that she felt he could fool rich women. This too made him fall even more in love with her.

While Malik and Brandy were getting their plan together Brandy's husband was doing an investigation on Brandy on his own. Though they had been together for what seemed like forever there was still things he didn't know about her. He ended up finding someone on Facebook who Brandy used to always mention from her childhood. He called the lady and once she gave him permission to come talk to her, he booked a flight. Doug had to catch a flight to Omaha, Nebraska to talk to Brandy's long-lost friend.

Once Doug touched down in Nebraska he got into his rental car and was headed to see Brandy's friend Tabitha. The first thing Doug asked her was how she knew Brandy which she shared the information with him. Tabitha then told Doug that Brandy was a good girl, but she had a very dangerous adventurous side to her as well. She told him that once Brandy's mind was hooked on someone there was nothing, she wouldn't do to keep them happy. She told him that was why Brandy had been all around the United States before she was seventeen years old. Most of the time

Brandy would run away from foster homes and hitch rides to other states. She lived on the edge and Tabitha told Doug if he ever did find Brandy she would be surprised. She told him that Brandy had so many ties to different states that she doubted he would ever find her. Those words took hope away from Doug, but he tried not to show it.

Malik turned on a song for himself and Brandy. They were up dancing while sipping wine and listening to a song called, "on the run." They had plans of getting Malik some dates on this night. Brandy gave Malik the run down on how to set up the dating site applications on the untraceable Trac Phone she bought for them. Afterwards Malik set up his accounts on the dating sites. Thirty minutes didn't even pass before multiple women got at him. His profile picture stood out more than any of the other men on the site, so he was a magnet from the start. Brandy told him they would choose who he went on dates with very carefully. She told him how some women on the site just wanted sex and that wasn't what they were after, they wanted money. Malik agreed with the love of his life.

As Brandy rested her head on Malik's shoulder while they danced to the music, Malik had a thought go through his mind. Though he tried to shake the thought he just couldn't fight the feeling because he was in love. He then grabbed the knife off the table without Brandy knowing and began to stab her. Her head was still resting on his shoulder when he began to brutally stab her. She didn't see it coming and shouldn't have felt the pain from the multiple stab wounds Malik put in her body. She shouldn't have felt the pain because he first stabbed her in the neck, so she was dead instantly. Brandy laid there lifeless as Malik looked down at her and screamed like he was surprised at what happened. That's when he started talking to her dead body.

"Baby, I'm sorry but they made me do this to you. I just couldn't fight it," said Malik as he laid over Brandy's dead body getting soaked in blood and still kissing her.

Malik wiped Brandy down with soap and water then put different clothes on her body. He went into Brandy's belongings and found a nail kit. For some reason Malik started to give Brandy's lifeless hands and feet a manicure and pedicure.

"I know your favorite color is purple so I'm a paint your nails purple. Is that what you want baby," asked Malik though he was talking to a dead body?

Malik talked to Brandy's dead body for hours before getting up and making a bowl of cereal then baking fresh cinnamon rolls. He sat in front of the television eating and watching cartoons. The Flintstones was his favorite cartoon, so he turned it on to get his mind off killing Brandy. Malik was in front of the television like he was a child himself. Though he was laughing and talking to himself he would still break out in tears every time he looked at Brandy's dead body. For some reason in Malik's mind he didn't feel like he killed Brandy.

The next morning Malik was ready to get things rolling with the dating sites. He sat on the phone all night talking to multiple women from the dating sites. He stumbled up on a wealthy white woman from Arkansas who wanted him to come have sex with her. The woman made it clear that she only wanted sex. Malik got himself dressed before dressing Brandy's dead body again for some odd reason. After dressing Brandy, he laid her back in the bed. Once he laid her down, he tucked her in and read her a bedtime story. After the bedtime story Malik left the cabin and headed out to Arkansas.

As he cruised the highway listening to music, he wondered what was ahead of him. Malik was never a person to have a lick of fear in his heart. He knew before long someone would stumble up on Brandy's dead body. He hoped the letter he left with her body would give her family closure after they found out she was dead. He had written a letter about how to get over the death of a family member and left it on her dead body. The letter was weird but read:

Dear beloved family of Brandy Middleton,

"As you may know, my name is Malik. I know all of you may be hurting at this moment, but there is always a way to find happiness in a sad moment. Right now, I don't know how to feel myself. Brandy was the love of my life and risked her life to help me. Though I did kill her it was the people that made me do it. She will always have a place in my heart. I want each one of you to know that Brandy was truly a dedicated and loyal woman. Many say that life is like a box of chocolate and I know why they say this now. You open the box and find pleasure in eating the delicious chocolate, but when they're gone and there is no more sweetness you find yourself upset wanting some more. In life it's the same way, people open their lives to you, and you enjoy it while you can. Once that person's box closes, you're stuck wanting some more of them. I'm here to tell you that memories last forever. When you think about the love of my life as I was the love of hers too, remember her for her smile and her passion to help others. When you look at others, she has helped in the medical field remember that person is a box that would have been closed if it wasn't for Brandy and I'm living proof. That thought should let you know she is still here and, in our hearts, forever. I know many are foaming at the mouth reading this letter, but if you were in my shoes you don't know what you would do so don't judge me. And to my beloved stepchildren I'll be watching you all grow up from afar, but just know I'm here if you need me."

Sincerely,

Malik

Malik drove the highway shedding tears while listening to certain songs thinking about Brandy. He knew his life would never be the same without her. He was on the mission that Brandy told him was a rock-solid option to get money. He was now making it his duty to make sure Brandy's dream of him using women for money came true.

The lady Stacey he met from Plenty of Fish was a doctor who ran her own practice from home in a ducked off area in Fort Smith, Arkansas. She was in her early fifties and had two teenage sons staying at home with her. Though in her early fifties she in no way looked like it and she had an outrageous sex drive. She was Caucasian, but ever since her elementary school years she dated black men. Stacey's heart was still healing from a recent break up and all she wanted to do was have sex constantly to keep her mind off her ex. When she came across Malik's profile, she decided to see what he was about. She never thought a man who looked as good as Malik would give her the time of day, but to her surprise he had interest in her. After talking on the phone, they agreed that Malik would come to her house the next day.

Malik was with Brandy's plan totally, but still wanted to figure out his own backup plan. That's when he called the only man on earth he trusted at the time. He called his best friend Fatboy. Fatboy was from a neighborhood called Brightwood in the Indianapolis area. Though they were from different neighborhoods they had been friends since middle school. Fatboy knew Malik for getting money and not taking any stuff from anyone. Fatboy didn't know the mind frame of his best friend but was going to be there for his boy no matter what. Malik never told Fatboy any details about what was going on, he only asked for a few favors.

Fatboy was the man in Indianapolis and had the hook up on anything you could ask for. Malik called him to see if there was anything, he could do to change his appearance. Fatboy told him he had the hook up, but he would have to go to Canada to get the surgery done. Malik told him there was no way he could go to Canada. After he said that Fatboy told him about another option. He told Malik that he knew someone who could do a simple plastic surgery job on him, but the simple job would change his whole appearance. Fatboy also told him that new fingerprints would come with the surgery as well. Malik told his best friend to set it up and said he would call in a few days to check the progress.

Malik pulled into Stacey's driveway. He could tell she was a wealthy woman by the expensive cars in the driveway and the beautiful house that was before his eyes. Stacey had an alarm system and cameras throughout her whole property, so she seen Malik when he pulled into the driveway. Malik was driving a white Ford Five Hundred. Stacey went down and greeted him while inviting him into the house. Her two kids were gone so Stacey got right down to business.

She pulled her pants down and bent over the back of her couch as soon as they walked into the house. She told Malik she wanted him to hit it from the back as hard as he could. Malik didn't waste any time before he entered her and to her surprise, he rammed his eleven inches into her ass hole. Though he had a big penis Stacey took it like a pro for about fifteen minutes. She then turned around and told Malik to sit on the couch. After he sat down she got on her knees and began to give him head. Malik's eyes rolled into the top of his head as he felt the feeling of satisfaction.

Stacey wanted to suck Malik dry. She didn't know him but knew she would have to get to know him because he had a big dick. As her head went up and down on his rock-hard penis Malik told her he was about to come. She told him to come in her mouth and he had no problem with doing that. As he was about to come, he grabbed the back of Stacey's head and rammed his rock-hard penis down her throat. His dick was hard like a steel rod. Stacey was dead almost instantly. Malik then got up and put Stacey's dead body on her couch. After that he took all her clothes off and looked at her naked body.

Malik now had a mind state that no one knew existed, not even him. Though a killer no one would have ever believed the lust in his eyes as he looked at a naked woman's dead body. He then just laughed and went into the kitchen to see what she had to eat. He found a container of Chili and helped himself to a bowl. Once he pulled the Chili out the microwave, he put

Sour Cream and Cheese on it grabbed a Pepsi and went to watch television. He forgot crackers so he got back up to get some.

After watching a few episodes of Law and Order special victims' unit, Malik went into his phone to find his next victim. He was still waiting on something, so he was in no hurry to leave. Though Stacey was an important woman her phone just didn't seem to ring on this specific night. Since she wasn't expecting anyone Malik felt he didn't need to be in a hurry. He found a few potential dates in the area, but he had his mind set on hitting the highway. Malik's mind was nowhere near his physical being at that time; he was totally out of it. Malik made his mind up that he would travel to Texas after he was finished in Arkansas.

Lilian sat there at Malik's mothers table wondering why she wanted to talk to her so urgently. Tammy sat at the table and looked Lilian in her eyes before telling her she felt like she would never see her son again. She told Lilian where she felt Malik's mind state was at in that present moment. Lilian listened to the news Tammy told her and felt she was rushed for nothing because it wasn't important to her. Calling her from across town for what she had just said was ridiculous. Tammy told Lilian they would have to work as a team to keep things together because she knew her son would never show up again. Tammy wasn't going to let what her son built go to waste. She planned to stay on Lilian's top every day about what needed to be done. Tammy had her own people she supplied in the streets and needed Lilian to stay on top of things so her supply would never stop.

After the ladies laughed, talked, and discussed business with each other for a while Lilian got up to leave. Tammy looked at Lilian as she walked away knowing in her mind it wouldn't be long before her son surfaced and when he did, he was going to hurt Lilian bad. Tammy knew her son better than anyone in the world; she knew the phone he bought her years before would come in handy at this time. No one knew about the phone, but her and Malik. She knew before long he would call, she just tried to see if Lilian had maybe talked to him on the low already. That was part of the reason for her calling Lilian over in the first place; she wanted to pick her brain.

The FBI agents were in a meeting discussing if they should air Malik on television or catch him silently. They all wanted to air him on TV, but Doug fought to not let that happen. He told the director of the FBI that airing him on TV would only put his wife in danger. Doug explained to him that he knew Malik and Brandy would surface before long. He also told the FBI director that he knew a way to find their location, but he needed a few more days to find it. In no way did Doug look like he had intentions of telling the director his plans so the director told him he would give him seventy-two hours to see what he could come up with.

What no one knew was that Doug had a tracer on every piece of clothing his wife and his kids wore every day. The only complication he had was that he couldn't find the device the locations transmitted to. He searched the house but came up with nothing. His drunken nights were never good because he always hid everything from himself. Doug knew from experience he would find it especially with him looking all over the place for it. Brandy was on his mind and he couldn't sleep knowing she had a warrant for her arrest. Once he was to find the device, he had no intentions to go to the FBI. He had plans of going himself to get his wife back and planned to tell Malik to go on about his business. Doug's biggest disappointment was not having any answers for his children. Without his wife around he didn't even want his children, but that was for him to know.

CHAPTER 6

Malik eventually carried Stacey's dead body into her bedroom and tucked her into bed. He then started to look through her belongings to see if he could find anything worth even a little bit of value. After looking through things for every bit of three minutes he stopped his search and went to lay in the bed with her dead body. He then turned on the TV and ordered some hardcore porn videos. After watching one for a few minutes, he went to her private bathroom and grabbed her bottle of Victoria's Secret lotion then went to lay back down. As the lady in the porn video moaned Malik jacked off while feeling on Stacey's dead breast. In his heart he felt it was weird but something inside of him urged him to do it.

After Malik pleased himself, he put his clothes on and headed to the kitchen to wash dishes. He turned on the surround sound and began to clean. He turned on an all Cash Money Records station on Spotify. As he mopped the floor someone entered the house. Stacey's teenage boys Zach and Lil Randy didn't seem to be surprised to see a man in the house. Malik introduced himself as Brian and told them he was cleaning up the mess him and Stacey made while she slept. The boys gave him a kind wave and went on to their bedrooms to play video games. They knew their mother would be sleep until the wee hours of the morning like she did every day. When they walked past their mother's door they glanced in and seen her in her bed sleep as always.

Once Malik got done cleaning he headed back into the bedroom. He found two firearms that Stacey had hidden. He put one on each of his sides. After that he got on his cell phone to see about any dates in the Texas area on Plenty of Fish. He found a few women online at the time and sent out messages to each of them. While waiting on replies he decided to walk into her walk-in closet. There he found what he was looking for, which was a safe. He examined it and seen it was a combination lock on it. Malik knew nothing about picking locks so he looked around to see if he could find any clues as to what the combination could be but came up empty.

Zach went into his brother's room and looked at his brother with a puzzled look on his face. He knew his mother usually had something cooked for them to eat on the stove every night they came into the house. At first it blew past him, but once he got a little hungry, he realized he didn't see any food on the stove. If his mother didn't feel like cooking, she would at least call them and ask what they wanted her to order for them to eat. Just as Zach began to tell Randy what he was feeling he heard a loud gunshot and seen his brother drop to the floor. Before Zach could scream or even blink Malik had grabbed him by the throat, and though he was a big seventeen-year-old he couldn't out wrestle the strong hold Malik had on him.

Malik escorted Zach to his mother's bedroom. After entering the room Malik pulled the cover off Stacey and the site of his mother's dead body caused Zach to pass out on the floor. Malik poured cold water on him to wake him up. After he woke him up, he told him he would leave after he seen what was in the safe. Zach hurried to tell him the combination because he wanted him to go. Malik opened the safe and seen money, jewelry, and different sets of keys. He then asked Zach if he minded him getting enough money out the safe so he could eat while on the road. After Zach told him yes, Malik grabbed a one-hundred-dollar bill and told him thanks before he shot him in the head.

After packing up snacks and hygiene items Malik headed out of Stacey's house. He left behind a hard-working woman who was so down on herself that she let any man who said the right words into her life. Malik didn't even think about it after he was done, it was like he would become demon possessed for a while and then go back to his normal self. As he hit the road, he started to freestyle rap to himself while listening to different beats on the radio. The person Malik once was didn't reside in his being anymore. Malik was now on a heartless mission that no one knew of, not even himself. He didn't know what his next move was going to be, but he didn't care.

Malik's mother answered her phone to hear the strange voice of a white man on the other end. He introduced himself as Doug and asked if he could speak with her for a minute. After she said yes, he went on to tell her exactly who he was and why he was calling her. He told her that he was getting closer to finding the location where Malik was at, but he didn't want to turn him in to the police. Doug asked her if she could go with him to talk some sense into Malik once Malik's location was found. He didn't know what type of person Malik was, but he didn't want to kill or be killed so he chose the safest route he could think of. Tammy told him she would go with him right off the top.

Doug went into his gun safe to retrieve his weapon and his locator device was sitting right with his gun. Though he was ready to take off right at that present moment he decided to go with his original plan and called Malik's mother back. She looked at the caller ID and seen it was the same phone number from Doug and answered the phone. He told Tammy that he found what he needed to find and if she was ready, he would head to Indy to get her. Tammy told him she was ready, and he hit the highway to go pick her up. Doug had the device, but the device didn't give a direct location address. The device only hit off towers that was in the area, but it would get them close enough that they would find who they were looking for. Doug knew he was in for a ride, so he braced himself for it by saying a prayer.

Malik was on the road again. Though he planned to go to Texas at first, he now had his mind fixated on going to Louisiana. He knew he could blend in if he went to the country town of Shreveport. Malik was in the mood for some loving from a country woman. Though he was just about to turn twenty-four he knew where the good loyal women resided. He also knew that hood rats resided everywhere, so he knew he still had to be careful. He couldn't believe the money in Stacey's safe didn't entice him. Malik was used to getting turned on by money, but now it was the least of his concerns. He didn't even have an appetite for food like he used to have.

Lilian was laying back in her bed wondering how things unfolded the way they did. She couldn't believe Malik had escaped from prison while knowing his appeal was guaranteed. Lilian knew that Malik wouldn't try to harm her, but she was still scared to see him again. In her mind she knew he would find some way to contact his children. So, she just planned to sit back and wait for it. Either way she knew it would be wise to cut off all communication with other men.

The next day, Stacey's doorbell rang. It was the father of her two sons; he was wondering why no one was answering their phone. After he knocked for about five minutes he checked to see if the door was unlocked. The door was unlocked so he invited himself into the home. He went straight back to Stacey's room and what he seen stopped him dead in his tracks. He saw his son and ex-wife laying there lifeless. He went to see if his other son Randy was at home next after calling the police. When he opened his son's room door, he saw him laid out on the floor in a pool of blood dead as well.

Randy Senior didn't know how to take in what he had just seen. He was at a loss of words and a loss of emotion; his whole body went numb. His children was his world and he did everything he could do to make sure they were safe. He knew Stacey was known for having sex with strangers and for some reason he knew that was the reason his children were dead. He knew what to do to find out what happened, and he was going to do just that. At that point in life he wanted to strap a bomb onto himself and blow himself to pieces.

Randy went into the office room of the house. The house was set up just how he left it before him, and Stacey divorced. He was hurrying to do what he had to do before the police arrived. He went to the computer and pulled up the cameras that recorded the house twenty-four hours a day. Only Randy and Stacey knew of the hidden cameras throughout the house including in the bathrooms. The two of them were weird like that; they got off on watching others use the restroom for some reason. Not to mention the many times they seen others go in the bathroom to have sex, snort coke and shoot up heroin when they had parties. This time the cameras came in handy for a good reason other than Randy and Stacey invading people's privacy.

He went back on the camera and seen Malik pull up to the house in a late model White Ford Five Hundred. He could see that as soon as Malik and Stacey got in the house, they started having sex, but when he seen her get down to give Malik head he was dazed after that. He looked at Malik on the computer screen and wondered how a man could do that to a woman who gave head as good as Stacey did. He seen Malik ram his penis down Stacey's throat and that's when his emotions got the best of him. He couldn't watch anymore of the tape as tears started to roll down his face. By the time the police arrived Randy needed oxygen to help him breath.

The police went into the house to start their investigation. They tried to question Randy, but he was in his emotions so much that he couldn't even talk. He pointed in the direction of the office room where the recordings were at and told the police he needed to step outside to smoke. The police looked at the footage and one of the cops immediately identified Malik. Though Malik hadn't been aired on TV officers still had a picture of him and knew who he was. When the cop who identified Malik told the other cops who he was, they called the FBI. After seeing the gruesome footage, the cops then knew what had Randy so hysterical. They knew they were in for a full night of work.

Once the director caught wind that it was Malik who committed the crime, he said the hell with his agreement with Doug and initiated a man hunt for Malik. At that moment all local television networks in every city was interrupted and a picture of Malik came across everyone's television screen. All radio stations were paused, and a description of Malik was given across every radio station nationwide. A full description of Malik and the car he was driving was given out across all the networks. The crazy thing is that Malik had no idea what was going on as he was listening to one of Brandy's CD's at the maximum volume cruising the highway.

As Malik traveled down the highway, he decided to call Fatboy to see if he had made any connections for him yet. Fatboy told him that he saw his face all over the news, so he couldn't help but to make any connection he could to help him change his appearance. He told Malik the car he was driving around in and everything. Malik was surprised to hear what Fatboy was telling him. He wondered how anybody would have known the car he was driving. He pulled over to ditch the car and decided to walk until he could find a car to steal. He was now in Lafayette, Louisiana and needed to get out of sight quickly.

Fatboy did give him good news though. He told him someone he knew in Mexico could do a surgery that would change his appearance. He knew someone down there who specialized in restructuring noses, cheek bones, and would also give him a new hairline. For the time being that was good enough for Malik. He walked the streets of Lafayette until he found a car. As soon as he found one, he was on his way to Texas then to Mexico from there. Malik knew of a way to get into Mexico undetected so getting in wouldn't be a problem for him. Mexico was a place Malik traveled to a lot because that's where all his drugs came from when he was still a free man.

As Doug pulled into the wooded area, he wondered how Brandy or Malik would know of such a deserted area. Malik's mother must have been feeling the same way as she grabbed onto her pistol to feel safer. They pulled through the woods until they came up on a cabin that was deeply hidden. The only reason they were able to see the cabin was because the lights were on all through the cabin. They then parked; both drew their weapons and went to see what was inside. They couldn't hear nor see anything, but they kept their pace going forward.

After snooping around the outside of the cabin and not hearing anything they both decided to go into the cabin. They slowly opened the door and as they tried to creep in, they couldn't help but to see the blood that splattered everywhere when Malik was stabbing Brandy. After seeing the blood Doug knew his wife was dead and told Tammy they should call the police because he didn't want to see anymore. Tammy then talked him into looking around more because she knew the place was small so it wouldn't take them long. Tammy stepped into the room where Brandy's body was at first not even knowing a dead body was in the room. After she stepped in, she turned around and hugged Doug with her tightest grip. She knew the body she was looking at had to be Brandy's. Doug then had a glimpse of Brandy's dead body and ran over to it as tears formed in his eyes. He stayed as calm as he could before he told Tammy they had to go. As they were turning to leave, he seen the letter from Malik sitting on the other side of Brandy's head.

Doug and Tammy both read the letter in disbelief. Tammy then knew that her son was truly in need of mental health counseling. The scene she was looking at was a scene that she never thought her son could create. She couldn't help but to feel sorry for Doug. Tammy had wanted a man like Doug her whole life. A man who would come rescue her from her misery as he was attempting to do for his dead wife. Doug called into headquarters and told them he had found his wife's dead body. They told him to stay there and that back up was on the way. At that point Doug didn't care what they were talking about he wanted to leave.

After the FBI heard the story from Doug, they posted on live television about Malik again and warned the public to never approach him if they were to see him. Even with Malik knowing that millions of people knew he was on the run he was still on the highway speeding. Not only was he speeding, but he was in a stolen car as well. He had the music bumping and was grooving to it like he didn't have a worry in the world. It seemed as if Malik was two steps ahead of the police without him even trying to be. The only thing he had to look out for now was roadblocks. In the south they were known for catching criminals after setting up roadblocks. Now that law enforcement knew he was somewhere in the south they were prepared for him. This was something that Malik already knew so he was just trying his best to get into West Texas so he could head into Mexico and become a new man.

Both Stacey's house and the cabin were swarmed with FBI agents, ATF agents, and many local police departments came in to help them. Doug and Tammy headed out from the cabin and were on their way back to Indianapolis. Tammy could only imagine what Doug was going through at the time. Doug had to eventually pull over to let Tammy drive since he couldn't see due to the tears in his eyes. Malik's mother couldn't believe the pain her son was causing, but he was still her son at the end of the day, and she was going to ride for him.

No one knew what was on Doug's mind, but he was prepared for his own personal mission. He made his mind up that he was going to retire the next day, leave his children with his sister, and go on the mission to find and kill Malik. Doug wasn't to be fucked with by himself with no backup. He was a trained killer. After years in the military and going to war for his country fear was just something that didn't register to Doug. He knew that if he was to dedicate his life to finding Malik, he would find him. Doug thought he knew what hate was before but after thinking about Malik he knew he didn't, he now had true hate in his heart.

Malik had made a lot of people sad over the few days he was on the loose. It wasn't that he didn't care about making them sad; the thing was that he didn't have any emotions for what he was doing. It seemed that ever since he had killed Sharp his emotions stayed hidden. He didn't know how long he would make it on the run, but he knew he had a mission to handle. He was on a quest to complete his heartless mission and wasn't going to stop until his mission was complete. Malik didn't care if he was to die, he just wanted to complete his mission first. He had enough ammunition on him to shoot and had the heart to kill so he felt he was ready for whatever.

CHAPTER 7

Malik arrived in Midland, Texas and his only mission was to get to his girl Erica's house. Erica was his connection to get into Mexico. Erica's best friend Frenchie owned land right at the Mexico and Texas border. The thing about the property is that Frenchie let the Mexican Cartel pay her to come to her property and dig an underground tunnel. The tunnel went straight into Mexico and no one knew about it but a few people. Not even all the members of the Cartel that paid Frenchie to dig up the tunnel knew about it. The only reason Malik knew about it was because he was very close to the boss of the Cartel after doing business with him for so long. Plus, Erica loved him to death and told him everything she knew.

While he was on his way to Erica's house he was pulled over by the police. He didn't have not one piece of ID on him so knew he was in a messed-up situation. The cop walked up to the driver's side window with his gun drawn. Malik sat there and put his hands out the window like the officer asked him to do. The cop didn't recognize Malik's face and seen the respect he showed him, so he decided he didn't need to be so aggressive. As soon as the officer eased up, Malik put a bullet in the middle of his forehead. The cop dropped to the ground and Malik got back on the road. When the backup officers got to the scene they pulled up to a dead cop and had no description of a suspect. They did know the cop was pulling over a stolen car, but from experience they knew they would find it down the road somewhere abandoned. They had no idea that it was Malik behind the murder of the police officer.

Malik ditched the stolen car about ten miles up the road from where he killed the cop at and went on to Erica's house. When Erica opened the door and seen Malik's face, she tried to shut the door right back in his face. He pushed the door back opened and hit Erica square in her face knocking her to the ground. Malik wondered what made Erica try to shut the door in his face and then he figured she had seen the news and got scared. He didn't waste any time with Erica at all though. He picked her up off the floor and carried her straight to the bedroom.

Once Erica regained her consciousness, she opened her eyes to Malik holding his dick in her face. As soon as she opened her eyes, he put his dick on her lips and made her suck it. After getting head for about ten minutes Malik told Erica to lay back so he could eat her pussy. Malik was now trying to be a gentleman to Erica. He gently licked around Erica's pussy as he used his finger to play with her clit. He just wanted her pussy to get wet and warm so he could fuck the hell out of her. She loved the way Malik made love to her ever since the first time they had sex with each other. Erica loved the way Malik's dick felt when it went inside her as she laid flat on her stomach. The way his body smothered hers as she laid on her stomach only made her love him even more as it made her feel like she was protected. She knew no other man could handle her thick ass like Malik did. To her surprise this time Malik wanted her to ride him. He never knew she feared climbing on top of his eleven inches and never would because she jumped straight on it and started riding. Malik now figured out that he wanted Erica to have his baby. She was a beautiful short thick Mexican and was down to earth. She could have had any man she wanted in her town but chose to stay to herself most of the time.

After Erica climbed on top and began to work her magic Malik was releasing himself inside of her within two minutes before she went down and sucked the nut out of him. Erica loved Malik with her whole heart, but after she seen him on the news and heard the details, she started to fear him. She knew better than to call the police so she figured she would just do what he said until he left. Malik informed her that he just needed to get to Mexico, and then he would leave her alone. Erica called Frenchie so she could set up Malik's route to get into Mexico.

After Doug dropped Tammy back off in Indianapolis his whole facial expression changed. He had no plan of ever returning home until Malik was in prison, he now felt death would be too easy for Malik. He figured he would go ahead and get a hotel room in Indianapolis then head out in the morning. For some reason he chose a hole in the wall hotel, but it fitted him just fine because he was in the mood to smoke some crack. Doug saw a lady who looked like a prostitute and asked her where he could find some coke. She told him if he wanted the good stuff, they would have to take a ride. It didn't take him long to think about it before he told her to get in the car so they could ride off.

The lady took Doug to a dangerous neighborhood in Indianapolis to buy the drugs he wanted. She thought she was frightening him because he was white, but what she didn't know is that he was also a dangerous man. After she came out from scoring the drugs, she asked Doug if he wanted some company. He didn't like to snort coke or smoke crack alone so he told her she could come to his room. Once they were in the room, they partied so hard that the police knocked on the door and gave them the choice to quiet down or leave the room. Not much time went past before the two had their tongues down each other's throat. After Doug kissed her and sucked on her titties for about ten minutes, he laid her down to have sex. Doug lasted every bit of ten minutes before he laid down and dozed off. The woman was happy he dozed off because that meant she didn't have to suck his dick. Her mouth was already tired from sucking dick all day. The next morning Doug woke up to an empty room. The prostitute had taken everything he had in the room including his ATF issued gun and his badge. When Doug looked out the window, he seen that she had taken off in his car too. Now with no wallet or anything else he didn't know what he was going to do. The only person he knew in town was Malik's mom and luckily the lady didn't take his phone so he could make a phone call. He called Tammy and told her what happened to him and before he could ask her for a ride, she offered him a ride. Doug was appreciative of Tammy; he didn't know what he would have done without her.

Tammy picked Doug up in a brand-new Range Rover. He didn't remember seeing it in the driveway but thought to himself that it was a nice SUV. The pearl white paint and five percent tinted windows set it off, and then the chrome rims put the SUV in a class of its own. Doug got in the Range Rover and told Tammy the full story of what happened. After he finished talking,

Tammy started laughing at him. He started to giggle too but really thought Tammy was crazy at this point.

"So, you than came to the city trying to get a piece of ass and some dope then got robbed? That's what these little girls around this area are known for doing. I'm just glad they didn't tie you up and hold you for ransom because they're known for that too," said Tammy still with a smile on her face.

"I really didn't plan on it happening you know. I had her score some coke for me and the next thing you know she was in my room having sex with me and you know the rest. I feel so fucking retarded," replied Doug.

"These types of things can happen to anybody don't act like a little punk about it. Just don't be so desperate that you let it happen again," said Tammy as she turned and pushed Doug on the shoulder while still driving.

They eventually pulled up to Tammy's house. This was a totally different house from the one he went to when he picked her up for the Tennessee trip. He asked her whose house it was, and she told him it was her house. Tammy laughed at him because she already knew what he was thinking. The house was in a gated community and every house looked like it cost over a million dollars.

"I'm highly impressed by this. This is better than any house I've ever seen down there in Kentucky," said Doug.

"Yeah, it's something I bought for myself so I can come somewhere and have peace whenever I want to," replied Tammy. She would have said thanks, but she took offense when he said he was highly impressed.

Tammy took Doug to an upstairs bedroom and told him to make himself at home. He looked at the room and thought to himself that her guest room was two of his master bedrooms. The thought of what she did for a living popped into his mind next. Not that he cared he just wanted to rest then get out on his mission. He now needed to get money wired from his family so he could buy two guns and a rental car. He figured he would drive the rental back home and then drive one of his other vehicles. With all the love Tammy was showing him, he wondered if she would just take rent money and let him stay with her. He didn't know what living it up meant until he stepped into her house and now, he didn't want to go. When Tammy came back to the room, she told Doug where the kitchen was at and told him to just get comfortable. She told him that he would see some things that said "don't touch" in the refrigerator. She told him he could have as much as he wanted of whatever, but the stuff that said "don't touch" was off limits.

Malik arrived in Puebla, Mexico and headed to an unknown warehouse to get his surgery done. He had

Mexicans with him from the cartel he had ties to, so he wasn't worried about no drama. When he arrived at the designated location the man doing his surgery already had a sketch of what he could make him look like drawn up. It was a full make over in Malik's eyes, so he told him he wanted the surgery. He asked the Mexican if he could do anything to alter his fingerprints and the Mexican told him he had him covered. Malik would leave Mexico a new man and this would help him complete his ultimate mission.

CHAPTER 8

TWO YEARS LATER

Malik was driving down the street with his music beating hard. His eighty-nine box Chevy was sitting up high on twenty-eight-inch rims. He had the wettest paint on the streets of Shreveport, Louisiana. To go along with the wettest paint, he was also the man in the town. Malik didn't force everyone to buy their drugs from him. The quality of his product was so good, and the price was so low that no one could resist shopping with him. He had a one year old and another child on the way. Though he did sell big drugs in the city he still went to work every day. His wife didn't go for him not having a job no matter how much money he had.

His wife's name was Tasha, but she knew Malik by Elijah Faulkner. Malik told her that he was from Texas but had ran away from his family because they treated him like an outcast. Tasha was an average twenty-year-old woman who grew up in the hood. She had a hustle side to her, but she had a working side as well. Her beautiful facial features, five-foot three-inch frame, and coke bottle shape would have you thinking she was an angel. Though Tasha wasn't all the way crazy, she still wasn't to be messed with. Malik was trying to get her pregnant from the first time they had sex. He loved her for some reason that he didn't even know. He gave her the only child she had and not long after their son's birth Tasha was pregnant again. Though Malik was the man in the streets he kept a pretty low profile for the sake of his newly built family. Malik and his wife both worked and on top of that Tasha had a cake decorating business that seen great profits. Malik owned stores, a rap studio, and three car lots out of state. Really anything they bought with illegal money was accounted for with legal money, which is why Tasha wanted Malik to leave the game alone.

After Malik's surgery was finished the Cartel gave him a whole new identity and told him to go for what he knew. He told them to give him five kilos and then he headed off to Shreveport from Mexico. The five kilos were gone within a day of him arriving in Shreveport. That's when he went to a hotel room and Tasha was the receptionist. They hit it off from the moment they looked at each other. One thing led to another and a week later Malik was moving into her house. Tasha helped the next ten kilos Malik brought to the city turn into fifty kilos in a matter of two weeks. They hit the game hard and slowed it all the way down once they met the quota they were trying to reach. Once they hit that mark Tasha told Malik she didn't want anything else to do with the dope game. Tasha wasn't a greedy person and knew when to leave the game.

Lilian went on living her life without Malik, though it was hard for her mainly because his children asked about him daily. She had another man in her life, but her mind was never with him. All Lilian could do was wonder if Malik was okay and wait for his call. In her mind she knew he was down in Mexico hiding out somewhere. However, she didn't want to risk going down there to find out so she just kept hope that he was fine and would return one day. She prayed that he would secretly send for her and the kids so they could disappear right with him. Her heart was all over the place and she couldn't stand Malik being away without her knowing his whereabouts. She felt that when he was in prison she at least knew where he was at, now all she could do was guess.

Malik's mother constantly prayed that her son would stay safe and not hurt anyone else. Malik did stay on his mother's mind, but she wasn't going to stop living her life. Doug never left after the day she welcomed him into her home. They weren't dating each other, but they helped each other get over their losses. They had traveled to every major city in the United States and enjoyed themselves every day. It was hard for them dealing with their losses, but they found ways to cope with the losses and kept moving in a positive direction. Tammy was mainly worried about her son becoming depressed and doing something stupid again. She was happy every day she didn't see him on the news again. After Brandy's autopsy everyone found out she was in the beginning stages of pregnancy when she was murdered. After Doug found out that news, he wanted to kill Malik even more. He knew it had to have been Malik's baby because Brandy hadn't had sex with him for a long time before her death.

Malik was on the FBI's most wanted list. On many occasions his wife Tasha sat right in front of the TV with him while he watched himself on America's Most Wanted. The surgery that was performed on him made him look like a new man. His wife just didn't know she was sleeping with a straight killer. A couple times she looked hard at the wanted man on TV and told Malik in a joking manner that he could pass for the wanted man. Malik would laugh with her knowing in the back of his mind, he was very well the wanted man. He was now with a woman he loved and was happy with his new family. He felt he had no reason to return to Indianapolis. He did plan to call his mother when time permitted because he knew in his heart that his mother worried about him daily.

It seemed like Malik turned into a saint after his makeover. Though he did still sell drugs he was in church with his wife every Sunday. Tasha was happy to have Malik as her husband and so was her family because she had been better since Malik appeared in her life. When Malik met Tasha, she was working in the hotel and still running the streets hustling in every way. Malik knew she wasn't the street type right off the top and that's why he wanted her. He knew she would be a powerful woman if she had the right opportunity and that's what he gave her, opportunity. Unlike her friends Tasha was raised by her father. Tasha may have done the wrong things often in life, but she still had morals and respect because her father instilled them in her. After meeting Malik, she was able to get the comfortability she needed so she could take her life to higher levels. They ran through the drugs like they were nothing and a lot of the money went towards Tasha's education, which she was now a CNA and going to school to become an RN.

Malik and Tasha's house sat on twelve acres of land. There was a thirty-foot tall stone wall that went around the perimeter of their land. Inside the stone wall there was an eight bedroom, ten bathrooms, and four half bathroom mansion. They had a pool house, a guest house, and Go Kart track on the property. Malik also had a full gym built on the property. The neighbors called their property the Faulkner's Estate. Malik and Tasha lived life to the fullest and were known for looking out for their community. They didn't really have to leave their property for nothing because they had everything inside their thirty-foot wall.

Both Malik and Tasha had friends, but they messed with every friend from a distance. They were all about each other and didn't want to let other influences break their bond, so they kept people away. Malik was also baptized at Tasha's church and became a youth counselor. Many children looked up to him and so did their parents. Malik's dark side hadn't showed up in a couple years and that was a good thing for everyone, including himself. He tamed himself and was never pushed to anger too much, so things were working out fine. Only thing on Malik's mind was serving the Lord first and serving his wife second.

CHAPTER 9

As they pulled up to the hall, they rented for their anniversary party Tasha and Malik were both greeted by many people who were congratulating them. Malik got out the car in a baby blue Canali wool suit with Salvatore Ferragamo Gancini Bit Driver loafers on to match. He had diamonds implanted into the loafers and no one could take their eyes off them. After Malik got out the car, he walked around to open the door for Tasha. She stepped out in a baby blue Oscar De La Renta Long Sleeve Illusion Gown with Christian Louboutin pumps on to match. Tasha also sported a diamond necklace that was worth over three hundred thousand dollars. They were shining on their anniversary night. Instead of being chauffeured Malik drove his brand-new Bentley Continental drop top which was off the showroom floor. They rolled in with the top dropped looking like they were celebrities.

Inside the party they had all white everything and paid to have mirrors put all around the room and on the ceiling. They had plenty of alcohol and food set out for everyone to enjoy. A live DJ was there with a mixture of music going from R&B to hip hop. Everyone partied and enjoyed all the games and raffles that was set up for the party. You couldn't have asked for a better outcome. The next day they planned to head to California for a Snoop Dog concert. They had a condo on the beach rented for the whole week in California. After the concert they planned to chill on the beach and get some peace.

Doug left Indianapolis to go visit his children in Kentucky. He wanted Tammy to go with him, but she told him he needed to spend time with his children alone. Doug didn't want to be away from Tammy for too long that's why he offered her to go with him. Doug was starting to get attached to Tammy and was hoping for a chance to be with her. Being with Doug never crossed Tammy's mind though. Doug made sure he smacked himself daily for disliking black people in the past. After Tammy took him around many cool and down to earth black people he said he had been partying in the wrong places in the past. He had a good time every time he was with Tammy and her people.

Tammy used the time Doug was away to think. Her every thought was about her son. She knew Malik being out on the run would eventually lead to disaster if he had the gift her grandfather said one of her children may have inherited. Tammy looked at all her children throughout the years trying to figure out which one of her children seemed different. She felt every one of her children seemed normal at first. Then after Malik started committing gruesome murders, she knew she was wrong the whole time. She felt in her heart Malik was carrying the gift her grandfather always told her one of her children possessed.

"Hello baby I've been," said Tammy with excitement in her voice before she was cut off.

She knew it was her son calling because the phone he left her with years before was the phone that rung. No one else knew the number, but Malik. She didn't even know the number to the phone herself. Only thing she knew was that she had been waiting on that very call for over two years. Her heart skipped a beat when the phone rang. She was happy Doug wasn't around when it rang, she felt her son had perfect timing.

"I'm okay out here momma, I love you and will be in touch soon. Tell everyone I love them, and I miss you all," said Malik before he hung up the phone not giving his mother a chance to say anything. He knew his mother wouldn't tell anyone about the phone call.

Malik had been going through some emotional problems over the couple years he was on the run. Before he went to prison, he seen his mother every day and now he hadn't seen her in over two years, and he stressed daily about it. It took everything in Malik's power to stop him from going back to Indianapolis. He was far away from his family, but he still had ways of knowing his family was straight. He also knew everything Lilian was doing, or so he thought. He only checked on their safety, so he didn't know nothing about Lilian's personal life.

Lilian was out doing her own thing. She was known for partying over the years, but she was never known to leave the house as much as she had been. She liked to sip, snort cocaine, and smoke blunts at home. When Malik first went to prison, she started to get out and party some to meet new people. After Lilian started going to clubs, she never went back to the normal life she lived when Malik was home. It seemed she couldn't stay away from the club after she went the first time. Everyone knows a woman going to clubs getting drunk only leads to them going home with different men and that's what she did. Though she only let a couple men come to her house and made sure her children never seen them. She made sure her children were sleep and the men were in and out when they came to her house. With the other men she went to hotels or to their houses if they stayed alone.

Lilian did party a lot, but you couldn't take away the fact that she handled her business when she needed to. She was starting to slow down on selling drugs and was looking for legit businesses to invest the money into. She just had a hard time deciding what she wanted to invest her money into. She was paranoid because she knew she was being followed. The thing was that she didn't know if it was only the police following her or not. She knew she could have been being followed by robbers as well. Malik's mother told her that she believed she was being followed because of Malik escaping. Though that made sense to Lilian she still wanted to stop selling drugs. It was like Tammy wanted her to stay in the game, but she wasn't going for it. Tammy told Lilian that if she did decide to get out the game to leave her with the plug and she would make sure everything was all good. They had built an unbreakable bond after Malik escaped prison and went crazy. Lilian had no family in Indianapolis, so Tammy was all she had and really all she needed because Tammy was an all-around woman. There was nothing Tammy couldn't figure out. Lilian wondered how Tammy could do the things she did. Especially when it came to her selling all the drugs she sold while having Doug live with her and not have the slightest idea of what was going on.

Lilian never liked Doug being in the house with Tammy and found it very strange. She wondered why someone would leave their children and go to another city to live happily ever after. She knew he had gone through some things, but she found what he was doing very odd. Lilian wasn't into the streets, but both men she married were deep in the game and she learned well. She figured Doug was only staying around to see if Malik would ever show up. Then she would get confused again because she remembered seeing Doug snorting lines of cocaine. Whatever it was that was going on she found it weird and wanted to stay away as much as she could. Staying away wasn't an option for her though because Tammy called her over every day. Lilian was really on the verge of leaving Indianapolis, the only thing that stopped her was the fact that her kids loved their grandmother so much. Everyone was confusing her including Tammy because she found her weird too for letting Doug stay with her.

After Malik and Tasha left the party, they headed home because they had to prepare for their trip the next morning. Malik ran his wife some bath water and lit candles. Tasha took off her clothes and got in their Jacuzzi tub. Malik sat on the side in his massage chair watching TV. Tasha then began to tell him about different ideas and other things that had been on her mind. She felt comfortable going to him about anything. Though Malik was only twenty-six he still had a lot of wisdom to give her. It didn't matter what Tasha was going through, Malik always had a way to calm her down and influence her to see things a different way. It was the same way when he got down on himself, Tasha would come to his rescue as well.

CHAPTER 10

Doug stayed in Kentucky for three days seeing his children. When he got back to Indianapolis his attitude was totally different from when he left. Lilian and Tammy were sitting at the table when he came into the house. He spoke to them and Malik's children, but something about his attitude was totally different. Tammy didn't feel no type of way about it, but Lilian didn't like it at all and was feeling uncomfortable. Lilian wondered how Tammy could look past it, not knowing that Tammy just liked his company.

Doug walked to the kitchen table where Tammy and Lilian were sitting and just stood over them. He stood over them looking crazy, so the ladies started laughing like he was trying to make a joke. There was nothing funny to Doug at all. What he was about to do was something he wanted to do not even two weeks after moving in with Tammy. He was living with the mother of the man who killed his wife and took her away from their children. The ladies had no idea what was about to happen next. Doug lost his mind but was trying to make sense of everything.

"Tammy, over the time I've lived with you I've felt at home like this is where I need to be. You make me feel a way about myself I've never felt before and I appreciate you for it. I talked to my dad today and asked him if I was doing the right thing by doing this and he said yes, so here it is, Tammy will you marry me," asked Doug as he got down on one knee?

"Yes," said Tammy as tears started to roll down her face. She couldn't say another word.

"Wow, this is amazing and the last thing I would have ever expected. I'm really happy for you guys," said Lilian as she sat there startled.

Tammy was at a point in life where she did want to settle down and have a loyal man in her life. She never figured she would be with a white man and surely not a country man like Doug, but that thought had changed now. She had seen so many great characteristics in him over the time he lived with her that she only felt right accepting his proposal. She knew he was a good man and she wasn't going to let color come between her happiness. After all Doug kept it real with her from the start when he told her he didn't care for blacks in the past. He also let her know that she was the one who changed his mind when it came to him having that opinion as well. She knew many white people wouldn't admit what he admitted, so she knew he was real. When he told her that she changed how he felt about black people she knew that was real as well. She felt he had no reason to lie or he would have never brought up the topic.

Lilian was feeling jealous about Doug proposing to Tammy. She wanted to move on with her life, but she couldn't without knowing what was going on with

Malik. Lil Drama was the new man in Lilian's life. He was a good friend of Malik's before he went to prison. Lil Drama still feared Malik, but when it came to Lilian, he felt she was worth him facing his fear. The only thing that made him mad about Lilian was that she wouldn't fully submit to him. In his heart he knew she was still in love with Malik. He told Lilian one night that if Malik came to him wrong, he would have to kill him, and he hoped she wouldn't hold it against him. She looked at Lil Drama and told him not to speak things into existence. She knew in her mind Lil Drama wasn't nowhere near ready for Malik.

After Tasha and Malik landed at the Los Angeles airport, they headed to get a rental car and went straight to the condo they rented so Tasha could get rest. They had been up all night, but Malik still wanted to go out and party. He looked at his wife and started kissing her softly. He then went on to undress her completely. Tasha laid on the bed and let her husband have his way with her like he deserved to. Though Tasha was still young she knew the qualities of a good man and Malik had changed her life completely for the better. She did whatever he wanted her to do in the bed. What she didn't know is that she was in love with a man she didn't even know. Maybe Malik had changed for the better when he met Tasha though.

Malik started to kiss all over Tasha's body. Her perfectly shaped Carmel body turned him on to the max and he couldn't fight the temptation to make love to her every time he could. He then put a vibrating device in the back of his mouth and began to eat her pussy. She tried to climb up the headboard of the bed as she moaned, but Malik held her closely. Tasha squirted all over his face like a faucet after only about five minutes. She laid there squirting as Malik put her leg in the air and started to lick her butthole with the vibrating device still in his mouth. Malik didn't get to put his dick in Tasha because she fell asleep with his tongue still in her ass. Many men would have been mad about their woman falling to sleep, but not Malik. He loved that he could please his wife with his tongue to the point where she couldn't take anymore. Though after she fell to sleep, he still got on top of her and humped her until he busted a nut. She was sound asleep, and he was on top of her lightly humping away and kissing her all over her face.

Tasha laid there passed out in the bed, while Malik looked at TV and took his mind down memory lane. He was also trying to come up on a plan for starting a new trucking company. Malik's mission was to become as rich as he could before he was to leave the earth. He watched TV and thought for a while before getting up to put clothes on to walk to the store. Malik felt it was a good night for him to catch a breeze.

Malik's mind was at peace as he walked the beach with his Gucci shorts, Gucci flip flops, and Gucci wife beater on. Malik knew he needed to find an undetected way back into Indianapolis very soon so he could see his children. He missed his children sincerely and knew they were missing him too. He knew he could trust Lilian but held back because he knew the police was still watching her. After seeing his story on America's Most Wanted, he knew they would be watching his whole family very closely waiting on him to surface. His plan was to hold off another year, but he was missing his children too much which made him start plotting. As Malik walked the beach he was approached by a young white couple.

"Hey, you're walking alone. I know that's boring come walk with us dude we don't bite," said the man of the couple.

"I'm cool bro, just getting a breeze off the ocean before I go in for some sleep. Right on for the offer though," said Malik as he tried to walk away.

The couple looked to be in their late twenties. Their names was Will and Patricia. They were a young couple who were swingers. One fetish Will had was to see his wife get fucked hard by a black guy. Patricia loved black meat so when he told her about his fetish, she was all for it. The only thing they had to do was find someone willing to let him watch. When they saw Malik, they figured they would ask him if he was down for the cause. After all they knew there weren't too many single people walking the beach at night who weren't ready to mingle.

"Dude my girl wants to bang you, only catch is that I have to watch. What do you say, do you want to give it a shot," asked Will?

Malik looked at the white woman and she wasn't bad on the eyes at all. She stood about five foot two inches with long blond hair. She had a banging body like she was a stripper. It was tempting for Malik, but then he thought about the fact that he didn't want to cheat on his wife. He knew he wouldn't be able to sleep knowing he cheated on his wife on their anniversary trip. Before another thought crossed his mind, the blonde got down, pulled his dick out his shorts and started giving him head right in the public on the beach. The only thought on his mind after that was that she knew what she was doing. That's when her boyfriend asked Malik if he was going to come up to their condo. Malik couldn't say a word, his eyes were in the back of his head and he was speechless. Once he got his composure back, he told them he was ready to go to their condo.

They walked for about ten-minutes before they were entering the couple's luxurious condo. They thought the condo would impress Malik and make him do everything they said. They didn't know that he had an even better condo and more money than they could ever imagine. In their minds they felt black people weren't used to having nothing nice. Their thoughts were wrong when it came to Malik though because they couldn't impress him.

"Not bad after all huh buddy. You get away from the roaches and rats for a while. Then you get to fuck a banging ass blonde instead of a bald head hood rat. I know we made your night," said Will as giggled and put his hand out to give Malik a high five.

Malik gave him a blank stare but let what the man said go in one ear and out the other. He knew the way most white people looked at black people and laughed inside at the man who was standing in front of him. Malik knew that the man probably didn't have a fraction of the money he had and surely didn't know that he would have killed his ass quick. Malik then took off his clothes as Patricia pulled out condoms and was ready to have sex.

"Let's get this party started," said Malik as he grabbed her titty with one hand and gave Will a high five with the other hand.

"Come on and fuck me you sexy black motherfucker," said Patricia as she bent over the table while reaching back trying to grab his dick.

"Just get ready for this dick you pink ass white bitch," said Malik as he picked her little body up in the air like a toy and began to fuck her hard from the back.

"Fuck me, fuck me, fuck me, oh my gooooood, I can't believe this," said Patricia.

Malik continued to fuck her hard from the back until she started to cream all over his eleven inches. As soon as she got her composure back, she turned around and licked all her cum off his dick and begged him to fuck her in the ass. He looked at her and was amazed that she begged him to put it in her ass because all other women ran from it. He was starting to think that this was truly his lucky night. The whole time he was already massaging her ass cheeks with one hand and putting his finger in her butt with the other hand.

"You sure you ready for that part," asked Malik?

"You just fuck me you black big dick fucker, you turn me on so fucking much. I want your dick in every way," said Patricia as she looked Malik in his eyes.

"Hey, don't get so fucking into detail babe, it's enough I'm letting a black guy with a horse dick bang you out in my face. Have some fucking respect," demanded Will.

Malik then picked Patricia up by her waist and turned her upside down. After turning her upside down, he began to eat her pussy. Her thighs rested on his shoulders as she curled her legs and rubbed the back of his head with her pretty little feet. Malik only wished he still had his dreads for her to run her feet through. He was a sucker for pretty feet as he fanaticized sucking on her perfectly manicured toes. Everything about Patricia turned Malik on and to think she was with a sucker who would let another man have sex with her in his face was ridiculous. Patricia was sucking his dick upside down so good that Malik's knees were starting to buckle. As he licked her clit, he bit off her pussy lips and spit them on the floor. She began to scream until he threw her headfirst into the floor while he was holding her by the waist. Her screams stopped as soon as she hit the floor because her neck broke from the force Malik used.

Will stood there in shock as Malik made his way towards him. Malik's didn't have to use any force with Will as Will stood there in shock unable to holler or run. Malik grabbed him by the neck with a firm grip until Will finally opened his mouth. He then grabbed a burning candle and put it fire first into Will's mouth. Will was so scared that he didn't even feel the fire before it went out in his mouth. After burning his mouth to crisp, Malik snapped Will's neck. He then went in their bathroom and took shower. Malik knew he couldn't go back to Tasha smelling like another woman. After his shower he cleaned up what little evidence was there and headed back to his wife.

Malik got out of Will and Patricia's condo without being noticed and headed back to his beach front condo. He stopped at the store for gummy bears and Hi C juice on the way back to the condo for him and his wife. He was on vacation and was about to have a good time. Malik moved on with his life like he never met Will and Patricia. When he killed them, he really didn't want to, but something in him made him do it.

The next morning Malik woke his wife up to breakfast in bed. Malik made them both a Meat Lover's pizza Omelet's for breakfast. Breakfast in bed was something him and Tasha did for one another on the regular. Tasha loved the fact that she had a man who could cook and didn't mind cooking. Men from where she was from felt it was a woman's job to cook so she was grateful for Malik's willingness to cook for her. The few friends that Tasha did have only wished they had men that would cook for them.

"Baby, what you than made us for breakfast," asked Tasha as she kissed her husband and told him thanks? They were both resting on the bed with their food on trays in front of them.

"I thought about something new last night and came up with Pizza Omelet's," said Malik as he smiled because he loved being the reason why his wife smiled.

He made them both four egg omelets each. Inside he had Italian sausage, pepperoni, regular sausage, bacon, and ground beef for meats. He put three different cheeses, green peppers, onions and marinara sauce in them as well. He served them with toast, orange juice, and fruit on the side.

"You always thinking of something baby, this is so good," said Tasha as she ate her food.

After eating they made love and planned out what they were going to do for the day. That was before they heard someone knocking at the door. Tasha got up to put on her robe and answer the door. Someone knocking on the door was out of the ordinary for them because they didn't tell anyone where they were going. When Tasha got up, she had a serious attitude and wanted to know who the fuck was banging on their door.

"Hi, I'm officer Mingle. Didn't mean to disturb you this morning, I do apologize for that. There was a brutal murder on the beach last night. We're just asking every resident if they would have happened to see or hear anything out of the ordinary last night," asked the officer?

"No, me and my husband had a long trip and have been in bed since last night. So sorry to hear the news though," answered Tasha.

Malik sat back in bed hoping they didn't ask him to come to the door. The officers didn't ask for him but did give Tasha a card just in case she was to hear anything. Tasha didn't want to be on the beach anymore after she heard the news of someone getting killed. She told Malik that she wanted to go home. Malik was happy to hear that she wanted to go home. He didn't know if there was a nosey person out who would have happened to see him, so he was surely ready to go. He knew from experience that you could sometimes think you were the only one around, but a surprise snitch always came from nowhere with a story.

As they packed their things Tasha seen the juice and candy Malik had bought the night before. She knew the juice and candy wasn't there before she went to sleep, but she blew it off. She could never think of her husband as a murderer. Tasha was always a person who paid very close attention to the details of everything. She could never expect her husband, but she had thought he was in bed sleep with her all night. In the end all she knew was that she was ready to leave the beach and go home.

CHAPTER 11

Doug and Tammy didn't want a big wedding or to go all out for their wedding day in any kind of way. They planned to go to the Justice of Peace in downtown Indianapolis to get married. They had no plans for a honeymoon or anything. They were both older and didn't care for the flashy things. Tammy had never touched a white man in a sexual way in her life. She knew that Doug would want sex and she was trying to figure out if she was ready to go white. She knew she said she would marry him, but at the same time she was wondering if she made the right decision. Lilian promised Tammy she wouldn't tell Malik anything about the marriage if he was to get in contact with her. Tammy knew Malik would never be able to come around again, but she still wanted to tell her son out of her own mouth. She knew Malik would be mad at her not only because Doug was white, but because he was Brandy's ex-husband as well.

Doug was feeling like his life was finally coming together in a positive way. He still thought about Brandy sometimes, but the memories of her was starting to disappear. When he thought about Brandy leaving him and their children for Malik, he somewhat began to hate her. Doug did love Tammy for what she had done for him, but he really didn't love her enough to marry her. Doug wanted Malik to lose someone close to him just like he had to lose someone close to him. He made a promise to himself that he would make Malik suffer when he saw his wife's dead body and that's what he planned to do by any means. Doug put his plan together while he was on his trip to Kentucky. He never thought Tammy would say she would marry him, but when she said she would he was happy he gave it a shot. He knew if she agreed to marry him it would give him time to plan how he would make Malik suffer. Doug had collected all the information he needed so it was just about executing his plan now. He knew where

Malik's whole family stayed, and he wanted to kill them all. He knew Malik was somewhere watching the news and wanted him to see his whole family dead on the news.

"I reckon you're ready for your future husband to take you on our last ride as friends before we become husband and wife," said Doug as he put his hand out for Tammy to grab.

"You better go milk some cows talking that reckon shit," said Tammy as her and Doug both started to laugh.

Over the couple years they lived together they had made plenty of laughable memories. Anytime Doug would say the word "reckon" Tammy would tell him to go back to the farm with that shit. For some reason this joke made them both laugh nonstop. Tammy was ready to give Doug a chance because it was something different and he always treated her with respect. She was hesitant about the sex part but knew before long she would give him the goodies. The fact that Doug always put her first made her admire him even more. Even when they were out to eat trying something new, he always gave her the pleasure of being the first one to try it. In her mind she called Brandy stupid for running off on Doug to be a fugitive with a criminal. She couldn't shake that feeling for nothing in the world.

They planned to go to the Justice of Peace the next morning to exchange wedding vowels. This was the first time Tammy would have ever been married and she planned on it being her last time getting married. She knew Doug had been married two times and wanted to make him happy so this marriage would be his last as well. Not too many people knew that Doug had been married before he married Brandy. That marriage was so short lived that he didn't find it relevant to tell anyone. He told Tammy without any hesitation though.

Doug was in law enforcement and before law enforcement he was in the military, which made him very observant. He noticed Tammy never went to work nor did she ever mention what she did for a living. Those thoughts made Doug want to start looking into things around Tammy's house. He put it together that Tammy and Lilian had to have had something illegal going on. Doug figured if they were still operating the drug empire Malik started then it wouldn't be long before Malik surfaced to at least check on things. When Malik surfaced is when things would get ugly in his eyes. Doug planned to kill Tammy, Lilian, and Malik's children, then sit and wait on Malik for however long it took, alone. He knew he wanted Malik dead and would go to any extreme to bring hurt and death to him. He was confused on how he was going to do things but knew he was going to do something.

Lilian pulled up to her best friend's house. Her best friend Cecy was a Mexican woman who loved to drink, and party just like her. Though Cecy never caused anyone any harm no one ever wanted to hang around her because they didn't want to be labeled a hoe. Cecy was the type to have sex with a man first and figure out his name second. For her to be so pretty she still didn't have any confidence in herself. Lilian didn't have anyone else to hang with, so she found Cecy quite fun to be around.

"Girl, we need to take a ladies trip. Fuck everybody else we just need us," said Cecy.

"I wish I could, but you know I can't do anything like that until the summertime when the kids are out of school," answered Lilian.

"Well summer needs to hurry the fuck up and get here then because I'm tired of you running around looking so sad. I want you to be," before Cecy could finish her sentence Lilian's phone started to ring.

"Hello," said Lilian as she answered the phone.

"Lilian, we have been made," said Lilian's cousin Hosea.

Lilian had never heard those words before, but she knew exactly what they meant. Those words meant that the drug operation was done. She knew in her heart the only way this could have happened was if there was a snitch. In her heart she felt relief but knew she had been spending a lot of the stash lately and that money needed to be replaced. Then she started to miss Malik again because she knew he would have had a plan off top. Though she still had money and businesses Malik always told her to never spend nothing she couldn't replace. She knew Tammy would be shitty about the news but knew Tammy needed to slow down as well. Before Cecy could say another word, Lilian was rushing out the door.

Cecy's pretty face was the cover of many fake and devious faces. Lilian had no idea that Cecy was working with the FBI to spy on her to see if she had any ties to Malik. They knew about the drug empire for years, but that was the least of their worries. They wanted Malik and wanted him badly. After they were to get Malik, they planned to arrest Lilian and Tammy. Cecy had been telling the police there was no trace of Malik. That's when the FBI went in and raided Lilian's family. Though the police didn't find anything, Lilian's uncle told his son to shut down the operation and that's when Lilian was called. Lilian didn't want to bother Tammy with the news since she knew Tammy had her wedding on her mind but knew she had to tell her. Lilian was already in her car heading to Tammy's house.

"We have a big problem Mommy can you please come outside and talk to me? I'm sitting in your driveway right now," said Lilian.

"This couldn't wait until after my wedding Lilian, you're trying to spoil my night," asked Tammy in a joking manner?

"I wish it could wait, but it's something you need to know right now," replied Lilian.

After Lilian told her the conversation couldn't wait Tammy put on her clothes and headed out to talk to her. When Tammy heard the news, she got mad because she thought Lilian had cut the operation off on her own. Then after talking for a while she could see the sincerity in Lilian's eyes and knew she was telling the truth. Lilian told her that she still had eighty kilos of cocaine at her house, but that was the last of everything. Tammy told her she needed the dope as soon as possible. Tammy was old school and knew she would have to flip the eighty kilos and save the money because she had been spending too much as well. Over the time that Malik had been gone Tammy hadn't accomplished anything, but debt. She had her properties Malik gave to her, but the rent she collected wasn't enough to cover her debts. She wasn't going to depend on none of Doug's income because she had an independent mind frame.

Lilian knew she could go to her side dude Lil Drama to use his plug if she wanted to. She knew he had found a new plug when Malik went to prison and seemed to be doing good. Even if she wanted to go to him, she couldn't though because no one knew what she was doing. Lilian kept her life private and the only people who knew her business was people who did business with her. After she seen how people ran their mouths for no reason, she knew to keep a low profile. As much as she wanted to leave the game alone, she knew she would probably have to keep some drugs moving. She had way more properties and businesses than Tammy, but just like Tammy she had high bills to pay every month plus she liked to shop. Lilian knew

Malik would have made a way even without drugs and that was another reason she missed him. Standing alone without a man was something she never had to do.

After Doug and Tammy got married the next day, they decided to go to the JW Marriot, which was downtown Indianapolis. Tammy still didn't want to have sex with Doug, and this made Doug turn into a mad man. Tammy was used to thug type men, but the way Doug went off was something different. This was her wedding night with the man who had never disrespected her and now he was yelling at her. She knew that the police would come to the room because Doug was cussing and yelling loud. Doug pulled out a bag of cocaine in their hotel room and started to snort lines off the table. The whole time he was snorting he was looking up at Tammy looking like a devil. Then he said,

"So, I guess you're too good for a line of coke huh bitch?"

"Bitch is your momma too good for a line of coke. Country ass Life with Louie built bastard," said Tammy right back to him without hesitation.

That's when Doug jumped to his feet like he was about to charge at Tammy and attack her. Tammy stepped back and pulled out her gun. Doug looked at her and laughed when she pulled out the gun. As Doug laughed in Tammy's face, he said,

"It was a test honey."

"What the fuck do you mean test punk bitch," asked Tammy with anger in her voice and her finger on the trigger?

"Listen I wanted to see how far you would go. I've been knowing that you and Lilian have a drug operation going on. I'm ex law enforcement, but I'm not a snitch. I'm sorry honey, just thought talking like that would make you think I was down to earth instead of always perfect to you," explained Doug.

"Doug what do you mean drug operation," asked Tammy?

"I see how deep in the drug game you are and know you can't say anything. I'm just going to show you I'm not a snitch. I'll show you first thing tomorrow. I'm ready to go home, fuck this place it's just a waste of money. Can't get any pussy anyway," said Doug.

"You sure can't bastard," said Tammy as she got up to grab her things and walk out the hotel room.

Tammy couldn't believe how Doug was acting. Over the years she had never put faith into a man, but the one time she did she now regretted it. She now knew why she was having a feeling something wasn't right with him. Doug did a good job in covering up what he really felt, but Tammy knew he was going through a difficult time in life. She was still willing to give him a chance because she knew that hurt could make a person say things they didn't mean. She figured she had given chances to men who treated her worst. She wanted to give him a chance just like she wanted the FBI to give her son another chance. They went home to go to sleep though Doug never got out the car, he slept like a baby right in the driveway.

The next morning Tammy woke up and Doug was pacing around the house in all black while drinking a cup of coffee. As soon as he seen Tammy's face, he said,

"Look I told you I was going to prove myself today. I've always had a fetish to rob a bank and I want to do it today. That way you'll know I'm a criminal and won't have to hide your illegal business away from me."

"What the fuck is wrong with you Doug," asked Tammy?

"I want to be accepted by my wife. I know you have something going on and I want in and want in immediately, so I'll show you I'm down," replied Doug.

"Well go make a fool of your dumb ass self and rob a bank then," said Tammy.

Over the couple years Doug and Tammy had been hanging they had never cussed at each other at all. It was crazy that all the bad things had to happen after they got married. Now Doug was trying to turn into a thug, but truly didn't have a gangster bone in his body. Tammy told him to handle his business, but never thought he would go out and rob a bank. She did know he knew something was going on with her and Lilian. If Doug knew too much, she knew he would have to die.

Doug was well experienced in law enforcement and if anyone could get away with a bank robbery it would be him. He had a dark side to him that no one knew about and the stress he had been going through only pushed him to the dark side more. He wanted to do something different with his life and the difference consisted of him going against the law instead of being with the law. He felt he had been on the right side of the law enough time and it was time for something different. In his heart he felt he needed to turn into a savage like Malik in order to kill a savage like Malik. The fact that his wife left him for a savage only made him want to be a savage even more.

Doug had been scoping out a bank on the east side of Indianapolis all along. He watched them like a Hawk until he figured out every employee's schedule. He followed the bank manager home on many days without her having a clue. Doug really got a kick out of putting in his homework on the bank. Now he understood why people ran the streets, he felt they ran them because it was more exciting than going to a regular job every day.

Sarah was standing at the teller booth when Doug forced his way into the bank. While holding a gun to her head, in a demanding voice Doug said,

"Bitch give me all the money and you better not put a dye pack in there or I'm going to kill you right now. If you think I'm playing, then let's fucking play bitch."

Sarah started filling the duffle bag that Doug placed on the counter with money. She didn't hesitate or think before doing so. Once she put all the money in the bag, Doug grabbed a big jar of Dum Dum suckers and dumped them into the bag as well. She thought the last thing a bank robber would want from a bank was suckers, but she didn't say anything. She almost laughed when he grabbed the jar of suckers, but then she looked at his gun and decided not to.

After Doug got all the money and suckers, he headed for the door. As he headed for the door a customer was coming into the bank. Doug hit him in the head with the butt of the gun and went in the guy's back pocket to take his wallet. The man didn't have any money on him, so Doug threw the wallet back at the man's head as he laid there on the floor. Doug then ran out the door to go around back to his getaway car. As soon as he got in the already running car, he put his foot on the gas to get away from the bank. Doug didn't peel out when he drove away neither, he drove away like he never committed a crime doing the speed limit.

Doug ditched the getaway car along with the mask and gloves he wore during the robbery. After getting rid of all the evidence other than the duffle bag he headed home. When Tammy seen the duffle bag, she knew he had really robbed a bank. At that moment Tammy knew Doug was the man for her. Tammy loved a man who could get out and get money no matter how he got it. With the plug for the dope being cut off she knew she needed another hustle, now that Doug robbed the bank, she knew what the hustle would be. If she could get the money out of Doug then she could cut Lilian off, which was what she wanted to do anyway. She was now thinking that her and Doug could go out and rob banks together. Lilian never wanted to be in the game in the first place so now she felt she had a new business partner. Doug couldn't have showed his wild side to her at a better time.

CHAPTER 12

Tasha and Malik got back home to a clean house after their long flight. Tasha was upset that their trip didn't go as planned but wasn't going to let it ruin her day. Malik on the other hand wasn't being himself. Malik told Tasha he was going to go workout to blow some steam off. She looked at him and told him to not let the situation get to him. Tasha didn't know that it was something much worse than their trip bothering him.

Malik got in the weight room and threw three hundred and fifteen pounds on the bench press. After laying down on the bench he benched the weight for twenty-five reps with ease. Malik was starting to slowly lose his mind because he was missing his family. The fact that he couldn't just up and go see them like he wanted to be was driving him crazy. He knew without the weights he was lifting he would have been finding a way into Indianapolis undetected.

On Malik's fifth set he started to fatigue. He was on his seventh rep on the fifth set when the weight started coming back down on his chest. Three hundred and fifteen pounds was enough to crush Malik, but out of nowhere a burst of strength came. When the strength came, he threw the weight back on the rack like it was the weight of a pencil. Malik got up in disbelief that he almost died, but when he looked in the mirror, he seen something weird. In the mirror he seen the image of a human, but his arms and legs had fur on them. And his arms and legs looked like those of body builders. His whole body had transformed even his eyes turned red.

"What the fuck is going on," asked Malik talking to himself?

That's when a voice came to him and said, "Malik you were born into an inhuman family. Learn how to use your gift and you will never die. We are humans, but we are not human beings."

"Please tell me I'm dreaming," said Malik as he investigated the ceiling where the sound of the voice was coming from.

"Malik you come from a strong Indian tribe and our grandfather left us with a gift that will be with our family forever, but only certain family members was able to inherit the gift physically. The rest of the family only inherited the gift mentally," said the Voice.

"Man, what the fuck? Show your face if you real I don't got time for no bullshit," said Malik as he looked into the mirror and seen his body transforming back into his regular body.

"Malik your mother is the true holder of the gift. We knew one of her children would be born with a special strength and gift but had to wait to see who it was and it's you. The only time your strengths come into effect is when you feel fear. When those guys jumped you in prison, you never feared them, so your strength was not revealed. Other than fear you will have to go into deep meditation to see what other way you can use your gift without fear. Your gift can make you or break you, so choose wisely. Never tell anyone about this, as you can see your mother has held her gift low key for years, we want you to do the same," said the Voice as a strong wind came through the weight room and left.

Malik couldn't believe what he had just witnessed. If he hadn't of seen his body transform on his own, then he would have never believed what had just happened. He wondered if this was the very reason why he never feared anything. Malik was happy with what he had just found out about himself, he was just hoping it was true. If it were to be true it would help him out tremendously with his new heartless mission.

He didn't think twice before leaving the weight room and going into his house to meditate.

Malik was halfway to the door of his house then changed his mind about going in because he wanted to be alone. He went to the guest house instead. As soon as he got into the guest house, he filled the hot tub with water and turned on the jet streams. After undressing Malik got into the hot tub and let the boiling hot water continue to run. He now felt like he was thinking with his own mind and he hadn't felt like he used his own mind in a long time. Over the couple years that passed Malik felt like he hadn't done anything using his own mind or body. Now that he was feeling more in control, he knew it was time to get to his mission. He knew what the voice said to him had to be true because he seen his own body transform with his own eyes. Now he was anxious to meditate and come in tune with his gift.

As Malik drifted off into meditation a clear picture came to his mind and the spirit began to talk to him, "Malik you are the last of a dying breed. You can follow through and complete any task you set out to complete. You must realize your great grandfather had one wish left before he died, and his wish was for his family to never fear anyone. He only said that because he was kicked off his land before he knew he possessed our special gift. We are able talk to our gods through meditation because our spirit is a force. Your blood line has pure Cocato Indian blood running through it. Whatever your mission may be, think of it being played out now and go for it. You have the strength now. If you ever find yourself in danger close your eyes and talk to me, I'll be here. I will never know what your mission is until I see you in action but try to always do the right thing."

After Malik's conversation with the spirit, he fell fast asleep. In a way he thought he was dreaming, but he wanted to see what this power was all about. He wondered why his mother never said anything to him about the possibility of his special gift. That's when he realized she probably didn't say anything because she couldn't let the secret out just in case, he didn't possess it. Right then he knew his life would never be the same as it once was.

Malik was awakened by a loud pounding sound on the door of his guest house. The person knocking was his wife's sister. She told him that his wife was being rushed to the hospital to have their baby. He looked her in the eyes and seen that her eyes were fixated on his dick. She not once told him to put on clothes while he stood there naked with water coming off his body. Any man who looked at her would find her attractive, so he didn't waste any time before grabbing her wrist and pulling her into the guest house.

"Bend over," said Malik as he shut the door behind him.

"Hurry up and put that dick in me, I been waiting ever since you started talking to my sister. I've been waiting on this day," said Tasha's sister as she anxiously took her clothes off.

She bent over on the kitchen counter and Malik gradually put his dick in her. He was loving the view of her body as he reached around her to massage her titties. Malik then began to slowly stroke her pussy as she moaned. She was loving every second of Malik being inside of her. Her pussy felt so good to Malik that he was ready to bust a nut in her to get her pregnant on purpose, so he would know she had to stay around. Malik then closed his eyes and asked the spirit to make him hump her as hard as he could. The spirits answered because he started to pound her pussy instead of humping her pussy, to the point of no return. He moved like a machine instead of a human. First her sister was loving the way he was pounding her, but the pounding got harder and harder. She thought he would stop because she felt him bust a nut inside her but didn't know Malik could go all night.

"Please stop Malik this shit is starting to hurt," said Tasha's sister in between moans.

That's when a smile came across Malik's face. He looked like an evil clown smiling in the middle of a magic trick. Malik grabbed her waist more firmly and started pounding her even harder. She collapsed on the floor as soon as he let her go. He stroked her at least two hundred times before letting her go. Malik had pounded her so hard that he broke her femur bone at the hip which was the biggest bone in her body. He also fractured the skeletal part that held her ass in place. She laid there on the floor crying. She was in unbearable pain and couldn't move at all. Only thing she could do was cry and scream for help as Malik smiled at her. Malik wiped himself off with a washcloth before putting his clothes on and leaving the guest house.

Malik got in his car and hit the road. When he hit the road, he had no intention of going to the hospital to see his child being born. Malik was ready to head out and find a new life. His feelings changed from being in love with his wife to fuck her real quick. Soon Tasha would just be a distant memory to him, and he didn't give a fuck. He didn't take anything that belonged to him except his car. He always kept a pistol and ten thousand dollars stashed in the car as well. He had his top dropped on his brand-new Corvette and had his foot on the gas doing the whole dash. Yo Gotti's song "Fuck you" banged from the speakers of his car.

Malik had his mind set on heading to Coffeeville, Mississippi. He knew from a few guys in prison that good women were there, and he wanted to try his luck with finding one. He figured he would start with getting a hotel room. His first mission after the hotel room was to see what hoes he could find on Facebook, Plenty of Fish, and Tinder. Though he was far away from Indianapolis his mind was still fixated on his mission there in his home city. He felt he would have never gone to prison if his guy had kept it real with him. He couldn't get that fact out of his mind nor could he get his fifty-year sentence out of his mind. Montario was the man his wife warned him about, and he was the man Malik was going to kill by any means. He couldn't believe he got a fifty-year sentence for keeping it real. He could have understood his sentence better if he had been a fake ass nigga who went down for murder.

After Malik thought about his whole situation, he knew he made a mistake when he escaped from prison. After all his appeal was a locked deal and he could have eventually sued the government for false imprisonment. He didn't know what came over him at times, but the feeling of inflicting pain on others seemed to satisfy an inner craving he had. Still to that day, he couldn't remember any of the murders he did vividly. He would be the calmest person one second, kill a person the next second, and then be the calmest person again. He didn't feel good or bad about the murders because he didn't recall them. He stayed with dead bodies so long because he felt they were just sleeping and would wake up any second. He had a mission to complete after escaping prison and that's the only mission he dwelled on. Malik now hoped his newfound gift would help him complete his mission, but he was in for a surprise.

Malik wasn't the same Malik he used to be. There were teachers at his old schools in shock after hearing the stories they heard about Malik. Everyone in school knew him for being quiet and shy around anyone he didn't know. The most he did in school was sell candy. He used the money he made in school from selling candy to help his mother pay bills. Though his siblings knew their fathers they still never helped his mother financially. Malik took it upon himself to go find ways to financially help his mother. When Malik met Sharp, he was five years old. He had met Sharp before then, but he was way too young to remember that meeting. Tammy always wondered why Sharp never wanted Malik to know that he was his father. Sharp would always drop money off to her for Malik plus spend time with him, so she didn't understand. Before Malik shot Sharp, they were super close to one another. Sharp never wanted to put Malik on with drugs because he knew he had a brighter future ahead of him. The only reason he put him on was because he knew Malik's thirsty ass would find it somewhere anyway. Sharp had a secret plan for Malik, that of course he only told his wife about. Sharp had put many properties, cars, and businesses in Malik's name for a reason. He knew that he would tell Malik he was his father. It was hard coming up with a plan on how to tell him so Sharp was putting stuff in his name thinking that would make up for him not telling him for so long. Sharp just didn't have enough time on earth to figure out how to tell Malik.

Malik's ride to Coffeeville was also a trip down memory lane for him. He remembered the night Lilian came on to him and him thinking they would be together forever afterwards. His only thought about her now was that he had to kill her for leaving him in prison the way she did. Montario was the first person on his list to kill though. Malik didn't know that Lilian suffered from the feeling of being alone, but he didn't give a fuck anyway. Before Lilian was a teenager her grandfather was selling her for sex. Her family was only heavy in the drug game because they started off pimping her out along with other women in their family. As a child Lilian thought it was okay to be sold for sex because so many families did it in Mexico. After she was able to move to the United States at the age of seventeen, she figured out it was all wrong. Sharp was the only one who knew of her secret and that's what made them so close. She only fell for Malik because he was there at the time and she already knew him. She knew she was wrong for doing it, but she was vulnerable at the time. Plus, she had no idea about Malik being the one who killed Sharp.

Others were always mentioning to Tammy that they couldn't believe the turnaround Malik made in life because he wasn't like that as a kid. Tammy was taken by surprise herself when Malik first turned into the biggest drug dealer ever out of Indianapolis. When Malik went on to killing, she was even more surprised, but didn't know he killed Sharp as well. She still had no idea that Malik now knew of the gift he possessed. Tammy never knew he was the kid who possessed the gift in the first place. She knew fear was the only way of acknowledging whether the gift existed in someone or not but couldn't measure it from looking at a person. She felt Malik didn't possess the gift because he was too close to Sharp. Tammy had put a curse on Sharp after the way he did her with Malik. She used a curse that would take true happiness away from Sharp for life. After she seen how happy him, and Malik seemed together she didn't feel Malik possessed the gift. One reason she didn't feel Malik possessed the gift is because he was too close to Sharp. Tammy was the main holder of the gift so if one of her offspring was to possess the gift, she knew they could never be close to a person she cursed. She went on years and years believing it was one of her other children who possessed the gift, but it was Malik the whole time. Now Malik was on a path of destruction because his gift was flipped to evil. Once it flipped to evil it blocked his emotions so he felt no sympathy for anyone and when he was in kill mode, he couldn't control his actions.

After pulling into the town of Coffeeville, Mississippi Malik got hungry and stopped to get something to eat. Mexican food was his favorite, so he didn't hesitate to go inside when he seen Po Boy's Mexican Cantina. The restaurant was a little quick stop Mexican food place, it was nothing fancy at all. Malik wanted to go inside to eat after sitting in the car driving for so long. Malik went in to order his food and after getting his food he had a seat at one of the restaurants picnic tables.

He sat at the table eating with one hand and was holding his phone looking up women profiles with the other hand. He started seeing a lot of women profiles when he turned on his location for Plenty of Fish. He chatted back and forth with some women while he ate his food before he left out the door. The only two things on his mind after eating was getting a couple outfits and getting a hotel room to go to sleep. He ended up buying clothes he didn't like at a country clothing store called Artwork by TopFlight. He just bought a few pairs of jeans and a few polo shirts. Malik hadn't worn anything but top of the line clothing since he had been in the game, but he said fuck it and bought the clothes anyway. After that he was headed to Econo Lodge in Grenada, Mississippi to get a room. There weren't any rooms available in Coffeeville, so he headed to a surrounding town. His plan was to get some sleep, but he also knew he needed to put a plan together for his future. He knew without a plan he would only fail, and failing wasn't an option for him. His dream of becoming the richest man in the world would always be his dream and that's what he was on the mission to becoming.

CHAPTER 13

"So, your ass than really went out and robbed a bank, what kind of other secrets are you holding? You don't make it to be a criminal overnight," said Tammy.

"I've always wanted to, and I did what I've always wanted to do Tammy. I've dreamed about robbing a bank since I was a kid and now, I feel a true fucking relief. I need to rob another bank as soon as possible I'm just getting started," said Doug.

Doug's adrenaline was going, he couldn't stop pacing the floor in the house. Though his mind was on robbing a bank he was still getting angrier by the minute that he hadn't killed Malik yet. Now that his adrenaline was pumping, he was ready to fuck up whoever was in his way. Death wasn't something Doug was fearing at that moment. He didn't care if he was to die after he completed his final mission of killing Malik or either bringing misery to him.

Tammy started to laugh and said, "you one crazy ass white boy, you go from being the head ATF agent to becoming a bank robber. That shit you snorting fucking your brains up Doug."

"I want the thrill; you can have the money. Once I rob every bank in Indiana I'll move on to other states. I could use a driver if you want to go, I promise it'll be fun and you won't have to worry about any jail time," said Doug as he pushed the bag of money over to Tammy.

"I don't have shit to do, we can ride," said Tammy as she started to look at the money in the bag.

Tammy felt getting the bag of money handed over to her was too good to be true. She had never in her life seen someone take such a big risk and then just give it all away. If he was ready to give it up then she was going to take it, but she was still cautious. Her plan was to swindle him out the money anyway, so him giving it to her willingly made her life easier. She knew she needed to watch him because the shit was too weird to her. She still thought he was just there to see if Malik would surface as well, though she never told anyone her thoughts.

"So why would you marry someone, and it seems like you're in self-destruct mode," asked Tammy?

"I married you because I love you. I feel you're down to earth and like I don't have to fake around you. I told you what I feel in my heart. I would have never come to anyone else about this, so know that you're truly loved and trusted by me," answered Doug.

"I know you're going through some things, but don't let it get the best of you. I'm here and I have tried to show you that these last two years. It's up to you what you want to do, but I just want you to know that it isn't about money with me. I mean I love money and it takes money to live but robbing banks won't last long. A job or business would be just fine," said Tammy.

"Well, I tried working all those years. I was faithful to my ex-wife. I gave her everything and more, but she still left me. So, I really want to know what it feels like to be a criminal since that's what she left me for, a stupid ass criminal," said Doug as he let the words slip out his mouth.

"Stupid ass criminal," repeated Tammy as she looked at Doug with a killer look on her face.

"I'm sorry, but at times I have thoughts," said Doug.

"Just don't let shit like that slip out your mouth again. Malik is my son no matter what. Maybe if you had of been fucking her right a stupid ass criminal wouldn't have had the chance to dick her white ass down and make her fall in love. She couldn't resist that black dick," said Tammy.

"Your son might have manipulated her, that's what criminals do," replied Doug.

"Get the fuck out my house and take your money with you, dumb punk ass bitch. I should have never let you in my house from the start. My heart for helping bitches always get me in these situations," said Tammy.

"I'll be happy to leave the house of a nigger and you won't have this house for long I've built a case on you you'll go to prison soon. Now you can see what your son felt while he sat in prison walls," said Doug as he got up to go pack his shit.

"I guess the little white boy mad now because his wife got some black dick and never came back home," said Tammy as she looked at Doug with a smirk on her face.

Doug jumped to his feet and then charged at Tammy. When he charged her, he knocked her down and ended up on top of her. He used all his weight to hold her down. Tammy start trying to push him off her but didn't have enough strength. Then she went on to say,

"Get the fuck off of me you pig smelling bitch."

"I wanted to wait to kill you so I could get you and your nigger son together, but I guess I'll go with plan B and kill you now then sit around and wait on him because I know he's coming sooner than later. I should rape you before I kill you because your ass has always looked nice to me," said Doug.

That's when Tammy quit resisting and laid there without moving under Doug. Doug was triple the size of Tammy and she had nothing coming when it came to be getting him off her. As he tried to suffocate her, her fingernail from her index finger grew into a long steel point. Doug didn't see it coming when she put her pointed fingernail in his ear and busted his ear drum.

The average woman wouldn't be able to get a man his size off them, but Tammy had a gift. Doug fucked up when he tried her. Blood started to pour out of Doug's ear as he began to cry and ask,

"What the fuck did you do black bitch?"

Tammy didn't say a word to him as she stabbed him through his left eyeball and then his heart with the same pointed fingernail. She started laughing as he laid there on the ground dead. The reason she laughed is because she felt he was stupid for trying her. Unlike Malik, Tammy had control over her gift and knew how to use her gift in more ways than one. She meditated daily trying to get closer to gaining full control over her gift. She knew once she gained full control over her gift that she couldn't be stopped by nothing in the world. She didn't learn of her gift until she was in her late thirties, but it came in handy ever since she recognized it. She knew it would have paid off more if she had of found out in her younger years, but she wasn't tripping. Either way Tammy never wanted to use her gift to kill anyone, she just wanted to keep her family safe and get money.

Tammy called Lilian on the phone and said, "Lilian I need you to come to my house as soon as possible, please."

Lilian had been out and about all day talking to private investigators. She wanted to put an end to the space between her and Malik. She needed to know something about Malik, and she wanted to know it right away. In the back of her mind she questioned if Malik was even still alive. Lilian knew Malik loved his children too much to leave them behind without saying anything to them. She knew how much his children meant to him and she knew Malik knew what he meant to his children. She knew they said he was guilty of murder in a couple different states, but she didn't know if that was true neither. She never knew Malik for brutally killing anyone, she knew him for being a protector and only killing if he had to.

"I'm your way now I'll be right over momma. Did you want something from Rally's I'm at the one on Pendleton Pike right now," asked Lilian?

"Yeah girl, bring me some loaded fries with extra bacon and a banana shake mixed with strawberry," answered Tammy.

This was Tammy's first time killing someone and she didn't know how to feel. She figured the loaded fries and the shake might make her a little more cheerful. Then in another sense she didn't even have an appetite. She planned to get rid of his body and go about her business like nothing happened. She was mad at herself for being a fool again for a man but felt relief that she at least got her revenge on him after his stupid stunt. Now it was just about getting rid of his body and acting like he never existed.

Lilian got over to Tammy's house and was surprised at what she seen. Tammy had left Doug's body right on the living room floor. Lilian wasn't used to seeing dead bodies just like Tammy wasn't, but she did know what to do with them to make sure they never surfaced again.

After the ladies ate, they wrapped Doug's body up in a old rug and Lilian called her cousin to come pick up the body. Tammy told her what happened, and Lilian told her she knew something wasn't right about him. Lilian told Tammy that Doug always looked at the kids like he had a problem with them and that's why she never let them spend the night with Doug there. Tammy was surprised to hear that from Lilian but knew that not everyone spoke up when they felt something like that. She was just happy Doug was gone before Malik surfaced out of nowhere.

Once Lilian's cousin left with Doug's body the ladies sat there at the table like they were lost for words. There were a lot of bad thoughts running through both their minds, but they tried to hold it in to be strong for one another. They were both at their breaking points in life. Tears were already forming in the corners of Lilian's eyes. Tammy and Lilian missed Malik and prayed to be able to spend a normal day with him soon.

"Mom, I don't know how much more I can take. All these killings are getting to me and I don't have Malik here, so I feel all alone with no protection," said Lilian.

Tammy got up to go put her arms around Lilian and said, "What's meant to be will be and it is hard, but

I know my son and know he will figure out a way to come back. This I assure you."

Tammy only held her tears back because she knew Lilian needed her to be strong. Tammy also thought to herself that there was no way she could cut Lilian off. She could tell Lilian was innocent and couldn't go on without her help. Plus, she knew Lilian would do anything for her. Every time she called Lilian for any kind of help, she would stop what she was doing and pull up immediately. Tammy couldn't get help like that from her other children, so she appreciated that about Lilian to the fullest.

"It seems like nothing will ever get right. The kids ask about Malik every day all day and I don't know what to say anymore. I went today to talk to private investigators so I can see if I can find him. I'm hoping I'm doing the right thing," said Lilian.

"Don't go to none of them son of a bitches about Malik. They could be the police their damn selves. If you want to find him, we will have to do what we must do, no outside help at all," said Tammy.

Tammy knew that Lilian wanted her husband back but felt she was stupid and desperate for going to a private investigator. She kept it to herself, but she was pissed off. When Lilian first said what she did Tammy wanted to smack the shit out of her. Lilian could look in Tammy's eyes and tell she was pissed.

"I know I was stupid for doing that, but I want him back," said Lilian.

"We will do what we have to do to talk to him, but let's figure out this money first. I have a duffle bag of money in the dining room right now," said Tammy.

Tammy and Lilian then went into the dining room to start counting the money. Tammy told Lilian the story about Doug again while they counted money and Lilian just shook her head. In Lilian's mind she was thinking that you could never put anything past anybody. Doug didn't seem like the type to rob a bank, but she had seen so much that nothing surprised her anymore. With the money sitting in front of them, the left-over kilos, and the money stashed Lilian knew they would have no problem with finding a plug. Lilian just wished Tammy would quit being so money hungry and think about something else in life.

As they were sitting there counting the money Lilian asked Tammy, "Do you think Malik is still alive?"

"I'm sure my son is still living Lilian," answered Tammy.

Tammy didn't tell anyone about the phone call she received from her son. After the phone call she knew Malik would be around soon. She knew Malik would never disappear on the ones he loved unless he truly had to. Tammy knew the risk he would be taking if he was to come around. She knew Malik would have to have time to think about how he would come around without being caught. When Malik called her, she felt he was already in Indianapolis. Tammy wanted to keep her thoughts to herself though.

"Why don't we just move far away together? I know I can never truly be happy with another man and you're the only person I trust. I don't even trust my family really and that's the reason I stay so distant from them. We can make a half a million in no time and just leave. I know we can invest and make something out of that. We can leave all of Malik's businesses and get our own. It's like I have no control over the things he had going on any way," said Lilian.

"We can move I will love that, but we are not just going to leave his businesses or his properties. He worked too hard to achieve the things he has, and all of his things weren't bought with drug money, he had legal things going on too," said Tammy.

"Malik had so many secrets because he never thought he would go to prison. I don't know where to begin with all that stuff, but if you say so we can make it happen," said Lilian.

CHAPTER 14

Malik woke up on a Sunday morning and did a Goggle search to find a church so he could go praise God. While in church he met a woman by the name of Jasmine. Jasmine was a lady in her early forties but looked like she was no older than twenty-five years old. Malik liked her yellow skin and pretty face. Jasmine wasn't a model-built woman by a long shot, but she wasn't one you would look over at all. She was interested in getting to know Malik and he had her impressed by their first conversation. After they exchanged phone numbers and had small talk, they went their separate ways.

Malik went back to his hotel room after church and logged into his usual dating sites. This time he met a woman by the name of Sherry. Sherry was a lonely woman from Coffeeville looking for company. She had recently divorced and wasn't looking for anything serious, she only wanted someone who she could go on dates with. She seen Malik's profile and he seemed like a decent guy to her, so she figured she may as well meet him. Her friends always told her she was too mean, and since she felt the same way she wanted to meet a new man. Malik's profile came across her phone screen, so she chose to see what he was about.

He pulled up on Sherry in his brand-new black on black Corvette. Malik wasn't expecting her to have company over, but a couple of her women friends were there.

"Don't tell me this is the man you just met pulling up out there in that Vette, look like you than hit the jackpot girl," said one of Sherry's friends named Tamara.

It was Sherry, Tamara, and Monique sitting around at the kitchen table talking when Malik pulled up. They were the type of friends who fucked each other's men and none of them cared. They passed their men around all the time. Sherry knew off top her friends would be trying to fuck Malik. He was attractive and they all liked tall men. Not to mention it looked like he was about his money. Malik got out the car and went to ring the doorbell and was greeted by three fine women on the other side of the door.

"You must be Jerome," said Sherry. Malik was going by the name Jerome Washington.

"Yes, I am and how's your day going beautiful? You're Sherry right," asked Malik?

Sherry couldn't help but to blush when he called her beautiful. He knew which one Sherry was because she looked exactly like her profile picture on Tinder. Sherry stood five foot seven inches and had hair all the way down her back. She had hazel eyes and perfect teeth. Her body was the shape of an hourglass and she had great things going for herself. Sherry's past hadn't been too good as she battled through homelessness and abuse. She overcame the hurt and went on to become an LPN. She also had an online business selling movies through Amazon and was making good money selling them. Malik was the first one to catch her on Tinder and she was only on there because her friends influenced her to get on there. After only being on there for about three hours she met Malik and her friends were salty at her. They were lusting after Malik the minute he pulled up in the Corvette. They knew Sherry wouldn't want to take full advantage of a man with money and really didn't think she knew how to take advantage anyway.

"Its fine you can step in," said Sherry as she walked back in the house.

Malik couldn't help but to stare at her smooth silky skin and admire the way her ass bounced as she walked in front of him. Sherry took Malik into the dining room to sit at the table. She didn't have any children running around so that was a plus for him.

After having a few drinks with the ladies Malik decided

he wanted to leave her house. He wanted some pussy,

but her friends were there messing up the game. Malik

told her he had something to do and left. When he left

her house, he checked to see if there were any other

women in the area and once, he seen there wasn't, he

decided to go back to his hotel room. Since he couldn't

find a woman on no other site, he went on Back Page to

see what he could come up with. To his surprise he

found a decent looking older black woman. She told

him she charged one hundred and twenty dollars for an

hour session and he told her he was on the way. Malik

was thanking Brandy while she was dead for turning

him on to a way to find easy women. Though Malik

knew he could have used women for money, he didn't

want to; his mind was on a whole other level.

When Malik arrived at the hotel room parking

lot that the hooker told him to come to, he knocked on

her room door. When she opened the door, she was butt naked and had her hand out for the money. She told Malik he couldn't enter the room before putting her money in her hand. Malik handed the money over and walked in behind her. When she got to the bed she laid down and asked him what he wanted to do. She started playing with her pussy with one hand and was squeezing her titty with the other one. Malik just stared at her. She told that his money only covered an hour, so he needed to hurry and figure out what he wanted to do.

"I want to do something a little different from what you're probably used to," said Malik as he pulled out two hundred more dollars.

"Well, if you're paying like this you can fuck me in the ass too and do whatever else you want to do," said the hooker after she took the money out of Malik's hand.

"I just want you to lay with me, I have a lot on my mind and just want to clear my mind next to a beautiful lady," said Malik.

"That's fine with me you're paid up so it's your choice," said the hooker.

After laying down for a couple hours Malik was ready to have sex and it seemed that the hooker was too. She had been feeling on Malik's dick the whole time and was ready to feel it inside her pussy. She laid down on her back and watched Malik as he took his clothes off and she was satisfied with the view. He then got on top of her and went up in her as she moaned telling him to keep going deeper. Malik was making love to this woman like she was his wife and didn't even know her. He loved the way she felt and was infatuated with the way she moaned. After slow stroking her for about an hour Malik started pounding her pussy real hard. He grabbed her legs and held them opened wide as he went to work on her pussy.

"Stop it right now what is wrong with you? You're hurting me," said the hooker as she started to feel pain instead of good sex.

"Bitch, I paid you my money and I won't stop until I'm done," said Malik as he humped her faster and harder.

Malik's special gift was starting to give him strength as he humped harder; he didn't know that sex was one way to make his gift come out of hiding. That's when he thought about how hard he fucked Tasha's sister. The only way Malik could ever have control of his sex life again was if he never thought about lasting longer before he nutted. If he thought about lasting longer when fucking a woman then his gift would kick in and make him pound their pussy. Many women liked rough sex, but Malik's sex was brutal when his special gift kicked in and no woman was ready for that.

When the hooker tried to holler Malik covered her mouth so no one could hear her screams. That's when he turned her on her stomach and started to hit her pussy hard as he laid on her back. She couldn't handle him and felt humiliated as his eleven inches hit her intestines with every stroke. Going off the first judgement she had of Malik she would have never thought he would be so brutal. He surprised her with his innocent face and professional demeanor. Malik was twenty-six years old, but still looked like a teenager in the face. His height was the only thing that would make a person question if he was a teenager or not. After he finally came in her he tied her up with the sheet he ripped up from the bed they didn't occupy. By the time Malik tied the lady up she was already unconscious. He tied her up to make sure she couldn't move, and he left the room.

Malik got into his car and headed to the store to pick up a few items he needed. He walked around the store to get the few things he needed and ran out the store with the items. He ran out so fast that no one seen the door open and close. The workers in the store all look at each other like they had seen a ghost. When they went back to the camera room all they could see was Malik standing in the aisle and then he disappeared in the wind. They were thinking they had just seen either an alien or a superhero. They let the theft go and said it couldn't have been real.

When Malik got back to the hotel room the hooker was conscious again and trying to break free of her restraints, which was unsuccessful. Malik then picked her up and carried her into the bathroom and that's where things got ugly for the hooker. Malik laid her in the bathtub and began to cut small cuts all over her body with a small sharp blade he had in his pocket.

After he seen blood leaking from multiple cuts on her he quit cutting.

"Please don't let me do this," said Malik talking to himself as the hooker laid there in pain and frightened to the fullest.

Malik then went to the front door where he left his stolen items at. He retrieved a bottle of bleach. After getting back into the bathroom Malik started to pour bleach all over the woman's body. There was bleach going into every cut he put on her body. The pain was so excruciating to her that she just closed her eyes and tried to scream. Her body was too weak for her to scream. After using all but a quarter gallon of the bleach Malik put the bleach down and started walking back and forth through the hotel room. He went back into the bathroom and when he seen she was still alive he picked the bottle of bleach back up off the floor. He then ran water in the bathtub after plugging the drain with her body still in it. He poured the rest of the bleach in the tub and drowned her in bleach water. The hooker had no chance of surviving.

After leaving the hookers hotel room Malik planned to go back to his hotel room and read scriptures from the bible. That was until he seen a man walking down the street who didn't want to move out the way of his car. Malik played it off and asked the man if he needed a ride which the man did say he needed a ride. Malik let him in the car and headed out without even asking the man where he was headed. While driving Malik hit the man in the side of the head so hard that he cracked the man's skull and killed him immediately.

"I bet next time you won't walk your punk ass in the way of my car," said Malik as he pulled over in a wooded area and pushed the dead man out of his car.

Malik decided to take a ride around the town before going back to his hotel room. He wanted to see what he could see, and he seen a lot of interesting things. He was in a country town but had intentions of bringing a city vibe to the country town. He rode past a city bus stop and seen a woman biting her finger nails off. Malik hated people who bit their finger nails off with a passion. It was something about seeing it that turned his stomach upside down. Before you knew it, Malik was parking his car, jumping out his car, and beating the woman unconscious in front of her children. When she hit the ground, he stomped on her hands and broke all ten of her fingers.

"Sorry lady, I just get a little pissed off when I see someone biting their fingernails off, it's a bad habit you should stop," said Malik as he ran back to his car and sped away.

He ended up seeing a bar and went in to have a few drinks. The bar was full of women and they all seemed to have their eyes on Malik. As Malik walked through the bar it was all eyes on him. The women looked at him in lust and the men looked at him with envy and hate written all over their expressions. After he made it to the back of the bar, he decided to have a seat and order a few drinks.

"I'll have a double shot of Grey Goose with pineapple and a splash of Sprite," said Malik.

"Wow, someone actually wants Grey Goose tonight. No one ever drinks this stuff you must not be from around here," replied the bartender.

"No, I'm from Houston, can't believe no one drinks Goose around here it's the drink of choice where I'm from," said Malik as he smiled.

"You need to get these people hip to the game then so we can sale some of this stuff," said the bartender.

"I'll be in town for a while I'll probably end up buying it out myself," said Malik as he looked at the pretty lady who came to sit next to him.

He realized she was one of the ladies he met at the woman Sherry's house he had went to earlier that day. He liked her when he seen her the first time at Sherry's house, so he was ready to see what was up with her. Monique liked him the first time she seen him and wanted to see what was up as well. She had just so happened to stop by the bar and after seeing Malik she was happy she stopped.

"What's up Jerome," asked Monique?

"Nothing really about to have a couple drinks and head out," answered Malik.

"Well, I'm heading out with you, and no I'm not just playing," said Monique as she laughed, but looked at his facial expression to see if he was down or not.

She couldn't tell but she knew she would know before long.

"Sound like a plan to me shit I'm ready to go now if you're going," replied Malik.

"Well, let's go then what you waiting for," asked Monique as she got up to leave?

"Shit, this not my city you have to lead the way," said Malik as he got up and put his arm out for Monique to grab.

The two walked out the bar and Monique decided to jump in the Vette with Malik. She knew it was safe to leave her car at the bar because she did it all the time. She left the bar many times with men and had them drop her back off in the wee hours of the morning. Her intentions weren't to spend too much time with Malik. All Monique wanted to do was get some dick and go about her way.

"I see you clean as hell; you are driving a Corvette and you look no older than thirty. What do you do for a living," asked Monique?

Malik turned down the music and said, "my father died and left me an inheritance, I invested all my money into Proctor and Gamble stocks and just been stacking ever since. I also have land that I rent out to Simon which they've built several malls on, so I get my monthly kickback from that every month as well and it's a real nice check."

"Seem like a smart man. You said you were twenty-six, what can you do with a thirty-five-year-old woman," asked Monique?

"Shit if you ready we will have to see I guess," replied Malik.

"How big is your dick," asked Monique?

"Something you'll have to see, it's right here," said Malik.

Monique didn't waste any time as she unzipped his pants to see how big his dick was. She didn't have time for no games. Anyone who knew her knew that she knew what she wanted, and she went straight for it. Most of her previous relationships didn't last because she was too upfront and most men from her town was afraid of a woman with that attitude. Malik was about to be in for the ride if his life.

"Well damn, hurry up and pull this fast ass car up to my house. Make a left at the light and it's the second right. You got a big dick let me see if you can work this big motherfucker," said Monique.

CHAPTER 15

After getting to Monique's house Malik sat down and they began to talk. Monique was drunk and horny and so was Malik, but they both just wanted to sit down for a while. Monique went and put on her night clothes with no intention of going back to get her car that night. Malik just sat back on the couch looking at Monique with a million thoughts running through his mind. All he really wanted to do was rest but figured there was nothing wrong with having a decent conversation.

"So, what do you do for a living," asked Malik as he looked at Monique and took a of sip his drink?

"Right now, I just work at the dollar store, I was a nurse, but they found out I smoked weed and fired me after I tested dirty for THC," answered Monique.

"Damn, but a job is a job. Where your man at," asked Malik?

"If I had one you wouldn't be here, but since you're here you can be my new man. My ex-boyfriend started getting deep into church and said he couldn't deal with my lifestyle anymore. His ass dumped me and went on with his business," said Monique.

Malik started to laugh, "For him to say that you probably do more than drink and smoke weed."

"He just wanted to change his life totally and I didn't want to be in the way. He came to me about changing and I told him I wasn't ready to change so he cut out, fuck him," said Monique.

"I guess that was the best thing for him to do, but what else are you into," asked Malik?

"I do whatever it takes to make the money, except sell my pussy that's off limits. Why, do you have a way for me to make money or something? I knew it was something about you. That's why I was shitty when you left my friend's house. She said she got a bad vibe from you and didn't want to see you anymore. I never thought I would see you again until I saw you at the bar. I guess tonight is my lucky night," said Monique.

"She got a bad vibe off me huh, shit that's her loss. I can't stand people who judge people they don't know," said Malik.

What Monique didn't know is that Malik had bad complex problems when it came to rejection. He didn't like what he heard when Monique told him that her friend wasn't interested in him. He wanted to go beat Sherry's ass at that very moment.

"So, what's up, what you got going on," asked Monique?

"I'm not going to say I trust you, but I will say I'm a trust my judgment and feel it's safe to tell you my side hustle that can get us both some money," said Malik.

"Well spill it," said Monique and she thought about the money she needed for her bills.

"Look I have a connection in Mexico, Iraq and Russia," said Malik.

Monique interrupted him, "Get the dope here and I can get it all gone."

"No dope involved, I'm a show you a whole new part of the game. I got immigrants from all three countries that are willing to pay top dollar to get into the United States. The thing is that most of them don't have money and I think I've found the remedy for them. Your house is big and if I get them to the United States, we can let them stay here. If I know they have a place to stay I will find identities for them to work under or find under the table jobs for them. After they get here and start working, we will hold all their money until they pay us what they owe us. Our job will be to find a way to make them become American citizens in the future. I know this may sound crazy, but we can make a lot of money once we get this shit started and it builds up. We just give them room and board and they will do the rest; I promise, they will do anything to become United States citizens. I have to work out a few more details if it sounds good to you then I'll start getting them shipped over here," said Malik.

"Out of all the nigga's I than met, I've never heard any shit like this, but I'm down for something new. All the old shit didn't work anyway. You smart though, shit you just seen my house minutes ago and already popped up with this idea. I love a man who can utilize everything around him," said Monique.

"Well, I'm going to make some calls tomorrow and we will get shit rolling. That's if you're ready this soon," said Malik.

"I'm ready for that and I'm ready for some of that dick right now too. We not going to catch feelings though because it might fuck up business and I like your style," said Monique.

"I don't put my dick in no pussy I haven't eaten first," said Malik.

Monique opened her legs and said, "Well nigga come eat this meal then."

Malik went over and got on his knees then started eating Monique's pussy. He was turned on because her pussy smelled like pineapples and tasted like pineapples too. Before Malik knew it, his gift started to kick in and he couldn't resist his urge. His tongue stretched out further and he began to lick her pussy faster and faster. She could feel his tongue at the bottom of her stomach. His tongue was so deep in her that he could have tasted the meal she had eaten in her stomach.

"Oh, shit oh shit, whatever your name is damn you know how to eat some pussy," said Monique as she moaned and held on to the back of his head shoving it into her pussy.

Malik continued to eat her pussy like he hadn't ate a meal in months until she came all over his face. He kept a hold on her while letting her cum all over his tongue and face. She enjoyed every second of it as he continued to lick her clit as she came. For some reason Malik took a like in Monique. Monique had her fair share of wear and tear in life, enough to make her somewhat of a risk taker. She was thirty-five with no kids. Her life pretty much revolved around her shopping, but she shopped for more things than just clothing.

She worked at a dollar store but had money coming from other places as well. She lived in a tri level house with six bedrooms, four and a half bathrooms, and enough parking spaces for every bit of twenty cars. She liked to spend her money on things like houses and cars. All her friends only worried about buying sexy clothes to look good for men, but Monique was different. Monique's mind stayed on getting money and she always stayed with a job no matter what money she made on the side. Meeting up with Malik could have been a good thing or a bad thing for her. It was all about how the cards played out.

The next day Malik called his connects in Mexico, Iraq and Russia, he told them he was ready for them to send the immigrants into the United States. He told them the way he set up for things to work out to see if they agreed with his demands. By the time Malik got off the phone with his connects from all three countries he had it arranged to have twenty Mexicans, ten Iranians, and ten Russians sent to him within a week. Within that week he had to have jobs for all of them like he promised to have upon their arrival. He figured that was where Monique would come into play at whether she knew it or not. All he had to do was find restaurants in surrounding areas that let people work under the table. Between him and Monique they would have to get everyone back and forth to work. For the money they would be making it was well worth the ride, the food, and the shelter him and Monique would provide them with. Malik wanted to start with immigrating men into the United States first but planned to bring women in on the following shipment.

Malik knew he could find dish washer jobs and other jobs for them that would pay at least ten dollars an hour. They were to get none of their money, their checks were to go straight to Malik for one year. After the year he would make sure he had a way for each man to become citizens in the United States. Once the year was over Malik promised to make sure the immigrants had citizenship, five thousand dollars cash, and a wardrobe to depart with of their own. During the year they were promised to not be treated badly as well and to be taught American English. Malik was lining up money with his homey Fatboy to get all the guy's new wardrobes upon their arrivals. They would also eat the best food on the market for the whole year. Malik wanted to do a good job with these men because he knew the pain they suffered in their countries. Anyone else would have been trying to get over on the men, but not Malik his plan was to keep everything official.

In all Malik would bring in sixteen thousand dollars a week from the labor of the illegals. He figured it was well worth the investment in clothes and food to start them off in the United States. He had five bedrooms available at Monique's house for the men to use as living quarters. He knew that wasn't enough space, so he cleared out the basement for more space. Though he looked for restaurant jobs he knew some would do construction and landscaping as well. It was all a win/win situation, but he couldn't let the neighbors see them at all. Her house was pretty ducked off, but he knew he still needed privacy fences. It was enough land to build even more shelter; he figured he would just take things day by day though.

In the days to come Malik told Monique the plan and she agreed to go along with it with no second guess. However, she did tell him she wouldn't stay in the house. With so many men living there that wasn't an option. Monique told him to give her twenty-five hundred dollars a week, plus pay utilities. Malik thought that was a sweet deal, so he took it and planned for his come up. This was just the opportunity he needed, and he could stay low-key plus out of the way of everyone. He estimated sixteen thousand a week as his profit but knew it would be more as time went on. He was ready to make his money and sit back like a retired old man.

Monique had to leave out, but she told Malik he could stay at her house. She had to go help her mom with some things at her house. Malik told her fine and assured her that her house would be safe. He needed time to himself any way to sort out exactly how things would go when the immigrants arrived. He knew he needed cargo vans to transport the men around, so he started looking on Craigslist for vans. In no way was he about to let anything get in the way of his plan. He knew he could go away and never be seen again if his operation went right with bringing the illegal aliens to the United States. He planned to go to the congested New York City and blend in with the many people who were there once he got things rolling in Coffeeville. This was a plan that was always in the back of his mind; it was now his time to bring it to fruition.

Malik was sitting on the couch watching the Cleveland Cavilers play the Boston Celtics when his phone rang. It was Jasmine who he met at church the past Sunday. She told him she thought it would be good to call and check on him. He told her he was doing fine and thanked her for calling him. She told him that she wanted to have lunch with him the next day if it was possible. He told her yes and they planned to meet up at the Mexican restaurant Malik first went to when he got to Coffeeville. Jasmine only wanted the company and conversation; she wasn't one to meet a man and go to sleep with him right away. Malik was getting comfortable in his new town quick. He knew before long he would have more than he had left behind in Indiana and Louisiana.

After getting off the phone, Malik put his shoes on and decided to take a spin in his car. He needed a little wind therapy to clear his mind and get his thoughts together. There was nothing to see in Coffeeville, so he got on the highway and headed north to Memphis for the night. He knew he could find something to get into in Memphis for sure as he did any other time he went. He knew he had to be careful in Tennessee because he killed Brandy there and knew the police was alert knowing he had ties to the state.

Back in Indianapolis Tammy and Lilian were getting things together for their new venture. They had found a new plug on the drugs and they were off to a good start all around. This time they put in their own work without Malik which made them feel proud of themselves, though some of the money to start came from Malik. Tammy promised Lilian they would move away like she wanted sometime soon but she really had no intentions of leaving. Malik was the one who got his mother used to the finer things in life. She knew the hard work he put in to do it and she didn't plan on letting what he worked so hard for go to waste. She had come from nothing in life, but her son changed her circumstances. Tammy didn't mind putting her life on the line to keep the lifestyle she was currently living. She knew if it came down to it, she could kill anyone who came her way stupid whether they had a gun or not. Her gift was always there for her whenever she was in danger. She had mind control over her gift and that made her calmer than the average person because she knew she couldn't get hurt. No one ever knew what she was thinking because she had the same attitude all day every day.

Tasha was in the hospital still trying to call Malik's phone. She couldn't believe he hadn't been to the hospital yet. At first, she believed her sister was lying about him raping her, but when he never showed up, she knew it had to be true. After all the time she had been with Malik she had never slept a night away from him and it was not a good feeling for her at all. They had accomplished a lot of things as husband and wife. Malik had showed her things, she never thought she would see in life. Tasha felt like Malik was running away because he didn't want any more children. Then she felt like he was leaving because he raped her sister. After so many racing thoughts she closed her eyes to go to sleep. She didn't want to wreck her brain wondering what she did wrong to Malik. Tasha was now thinking she moved way to fast with Malik. She really didn't know him and was now starting to question the story about why he never talked to not even one person in his family. It was like he came out of nowhere and then disappeared into nowhere a couple years later. She knew she needed to find out what she could about Malik and if nothing else put him on child support. She refused to let him escape his responsibility of taking care of the children he helped her make. The day at the beach for their anniversary was on her mind as well. She knew for sure Malik had been out on the beach the night the murders happened. She was now wondering why he kept it a secret.

CHAPTER 16

A few months had gone by and Malik's operation with Monique was going just fine. Monique had moved out of her house as planned and Malik was running the grounds very strategically. All the men were happy with their living situations. Malik left one bedroom vacant and let the men take turns using the room whenever he brought hookers for the men to have sex. He let the men pay out of the money they worked for even though it wasn't part of the deal from the beginning, he knew he couldn't go without pussy, so he didn't make them neither. He wanted the men to feel as comfortable as possible. Without them he wouldn't have been making the money he was making so he showed his appreciation in every way. After he was done with these forty men, he planned to bring forty more and do the same thing over again. He planned to change his location every time a new set of immigrants came into the United States though. He also planned to get a bigger property so he could try giving the men their own rooms when the next batch come into the United States.

Malik sold his Corvette and bought a brand-new Camaro. He figured he would get him something more low-key than the Vette but still get something fast. Him and Monique still had sex here and there, but they were business partners before anything. Malik mainly spent his time with Jasmine who he met at church. They continued to go to church and take trips on their spare time. Jasmine hadn't had sex with Malik the whole time they had been kicking it and he still enjoyed every minute they spent together like it was the best sex in the world.

Malik dropped Jasmine off at work one night and decided he wanted to go for a walk at a local park before going back home. After leaving the park and thinking hard on what his next move would be, he made a stop. It had been something on his mind for the last few weeks and he wanted to see if a statement he heard was true. He stepped out his car and walked to the door to ring the doorbell.

"Who is it," said a man's voice on the other side of the door?

"It's your neighbor your dogs are loose in my yard," said Malik.

The man then opened the door and stood face to face with Malik. Malik didn't waste any time before stabbing the man multiple times. Malik stabbed him in the throat as well as many other places. The man didn't have even a slight chance of staying alive. The man dropped dead right there at the doorway and Malik ran from the murder scene. Malik could hear a woman's voice from the back of the house asking what was going on before he ran from the scene. When she finally got to the front door she started screaming as she looked at her sex partner laying there dead. She picked up the phone and called the police. She had no idea who it was that killed him, but she was grateful whoever it was didn't come in the house and kill her as well.

Malik had wanted to kill Sherry ever since he found out she wasn't interested in dating him. He hated rejection and he felt he did nothing wrong to her, so he wanted her to die. Her male friend was the one who answered the door, so Malik killed him. Sherry would just have to wait on another date to receive her death sentence. He had it in his mind that everyone who caused him pain would be repaid by death and Sherry was one of them. She was very lucky she wasn't the one who answered the door. Malik was playing for keeps in every way in the game.

He got back to his house and took a shower. After the shower he turned on the TV to watch until he went to sleep. To his surprise he was on the news.

There was a worldwide alert featuring him as the suspect. They not only had his old picture before his surgery, but they had his new picture too. He could see his wife Tasha on the TV screen telling the news caster everything she knew about who she thought was Elijah Faulkner. His jaws dropped when he seen what was going on. They also had him the suspect for the murders of the young couple in California and a person of interest in the murder of a cop. Malik was lucky to be in Coffeeville for the time he had been there without the woman he attacked at the bus stop identifying him. After all he was in a small town and word did travel fast. The murder he committed in the hotel had never came up neither, but he knew after people seen him on the news, he would be held responsible for it all.

Tasha wasn't going to take no for an answer when it came to her finding Malik. She told her sister to do the DNA rape kit test to see if Malik's sperm was in her. The results came back belonging to Malik. After looking at the picture of Malik long enough she could see the man she thought was Elijah was in fact Malik. She didn't tell no one about her and Malik's money stashed or anything else they invested into. After seeing that Malik was a dangerous man, Tasha gathered all the money put away and told her family they were leaving town. Malik had left enough money for her to build from and be set for life. She just wanted to go because she figured he would be back sometime, and she didn't want to be there when he came back. She knew he would want to kill her for snitching about the murders in California. When she came forward with the information about their trip to California, they linked him to the murders. The investigators showed pictures of Malik's new disguise to people who were on the beach the night of the murders. When Malik was walking with the Will and Patricia there was an older couple on their balcony looking right at them, but they never came forward. They wanted to mind their own business because that's what they were taught to do growing up in Chicago. After they seen the one hundred-thousand-dollar reward for Malik they changed their minds though. Malik was now wanted for brutal murders all over the United States.

When Lilian and Tammy seen the news, their hearts skipped a beat. They were relieved that Malik was still alive, but they couldn't believe the things people were saying he did. Tammy and Lilian both knew that Malik would make the police kill him before he let them arrest him. It hurt them but they knew Malik would rather die than spend his life in prison. Lilian told Tammy she could have the whole drug operation and she would be leaving for Mexico within a week. Lilian had enough of the foolishness and needed to go far away to forget about Malik and Sharp. None of the men she had slept with made her want to stay in Indianapolis anymore, so she was preparing to leave the United States for good.

Malik called Monique on the phone and told her to hold things down because there was something's he needed to go handle for a while. She told him she saw him on the news but assured him she would never snitch on him. She also told him she would make sure he got his money and to stay safe because the police wanted to kill him. No one knew what they had going on in Coffeeville but them and Malik was glad he put Monique on his team. Malik had some trust in Monique so he told her he would be in touch soon. He got in a pickup truck he had put away and hit the road. He knew his time was ticking but there was a couple things he had to do before he was caught. In no way was he going to let Tasha slide with snitching on him. He thought she loved him enough to at least not to tell the police about their trip to the beach. He felt she was trying to put him in prison for life, so he planned to take her life as well.

CHAPTER 17

For the first time in Malik's life he was starting to panic. He knew he needed to get away from Coffeeville and he had to do it fast. Malik decided to take his time and think everything out before going on his next mission. He decided to meet up with a woman he met on Facebook. The woman's name was Destiny. She was in her late thirties and felt it was cool for Malik to stop by since she had been talking to him for about two months. His profile looked okay to her so she had no reason to refuse him when he asked if he could stop by her house. He told her he was in Shreveport about to pass through her city and wanted to take her out to eat. Destiny lived in Louisiana, but she stayed in a city called Rayville right off interstate twenty. Rayville was a small city and Destiny was a small-minded woman. Malik's only goal was to see if she could be of any value to him while he was on his mission.

Malik pulled up to Destiny's house in a ducked off area. Everything around her house looked like raggedy farmland though her house was nice. He asked her if she wanted to go out to eat, she told him yes then got in his truck and they headed out to find something to eat. They talked the whole ride while finding something to eat. Destiny took him to a restaurant called Big John's Steak and Seafood. When Malik got out the car and smelled the food, he was ready to go into the restaurant and try some of the delicious smelling food. They went inside and had a seat until their waitress came to take their orders.

After they got done eating, they went back to Destiny's house. They talked more and had a sip of wine. Destiny wasn't interested in Malik sexually in no type of way. She just liked his company and she had never really kicked it with a city man before. She was feeling Malik's swag, but not enough to give up her pussy on the first date. Malik seen she wasn't trying to come off no pussy but still tried to get her in bed. She told him she would rather get to know him first. This made him look at Destiny and give her major respect. For the first time on his rampage he didn't kill a woman he met on a dating site. Malik got up and left her house without saying another word. She thought he was mad because she didn't want to have sex, but just didn't know she had just escaped death.

When Malik left her house, he wrecked his mind trying to figure out where he was going to go next. He decided to go to Atlanta to have some fun and fuck some strippers. He stopped to get gas before getting on the highway. Malik was wanted for murder in multiple different states and had nothing to lose so he figured he would have some fun. He tried to come up with a plan to get off the case but knew that even an insanity plea wouldn't get him off the cases. He knew he would be sentenced to life in prison so turning himself in to the police wasn't an option. His mind was on having fun and that's what he was going to do.

Back in Indianapolis, everyone who knew Malik was very upset with him. They couldn't believe he went from being a thug type hood nigga to a social media serial killer. Many of his homeboys who once looked up to him now thought he was a lame ass buster. The main thing they said was that hood niggas didn't go around committing those types of crimes. Even his homeboy Fatboy was surprised, but he didn't believe Malik committed the crimes. Either way everyone knew they would never see Malik again as a free man or even alive for that matter.

Lilian was watching the news again when she seen Tasha the so-called wife of Malik's on a live news press conference. Tasha told the reporter that her and Malik had been together for about two years and she had just had their second child. They showed two pictures of Malik again and then told everyone that if he changed his appearance once he would do it again. They warned that it seemed like he was linking up with many women from social dating sites. Randy the ex-husband of the woman Malik killed in Arkansas told authorities that was how his ex-wife met Malik. She was known for linking up with men from chat lines and he knew it was the way she met Malik. The reporters had a lot of information about Malik and told a gruesome story of his character.

Lilian couldn't believe what she was seeing on the news. Though she was wrong for being sexually active with some of Malik's friends she would have never married another man. She seen some of Malik's wedding pictures with Tasha on the news and felt betrayed. She was hurt that he could get married and have kids while moving on like she never existed. She was ready to go to Mexico right that second. She called Tammy and told her she was leaving Indianapolis for good that day. Her feelings were crushed by the news she seen. When she told Malik, she was leaving him while he was in prison it was only because she was lost. She thought he would have understood the pain she was going through with him being in prison. She still planned to have his back while he did his time but was confused.

Tammy told her on the phone that she needed to quit being so soft. She told Lilian that she was out cheating just like Malik was cheating. She also told Lilian that it didn't matter if she didn't get married on him or not cheating was still cheating, so she was as guilty as Malik. Tammy told her to give it a few days before making her final decision on leaving Indianapolis for good. Tammy didn't have no one except her other children and they were too caught up in their own lives to keep up with Tammy's business. When she had gotten married to Doug none of her children knew about the marriage. Tammy really looked at Lilian as a real daughter just as Lilian looked at Tammy as a real mother. Tammy wouldn't have cared about anyone else leaving but she loved Lilian like a daughter and knew she would go crazy without her presence. Tammy then told Lilian to come over and have a talk with her.

Randy back in Arkansas was trying to figure out where Malik was at without the police being involved. He didn't plan for the police to take Malik into custody. Randy wanted to make Malik suffer for what he did to his children. Randy wanted to murder Malik's children just the way Malik had murdered his children. He knew about Malik's family in Shreveport and in Indianapolis, he was just deciding where he would go first. He wasn't fearing shit, he was only seeking revenge on a heartless bastard.

CHAPTER 18

Three days later Malik was back in Indianapolis. After going to Atlanta, he decided he wanted to go see his family for one last time as a free man. He met a woman in Norcross, Georgia who was very gullible. She let Malik drive off in her brand-new Tesla. She was a woman with money and didn't mind paying for good sex. It was right up Malik's alley at this time because he wanted another vehicle anyway. Though she let him use the car he still locked her in her deep freezer before he left her house. He turned it up to its coldest setting and cut out to head to Indianapolis. He felt she was cool, but he couldn't take a chance of her seeing the news and reporting him to the police.

Malik played music as he cruised his city that he hadn't seen in years. He drove past all the places he used to hang as he drifted down memory lane. His favorite song by a local rapper named Lil P had the speakers in the Tesla banging. Malik was grooving to the music but calmed down quickly after he remembered he was on the run. He wanted to see his family, but he had one mission to complete first. He couldn't hold back the tears that rolled down his face. He really missed his life and he wanted to kill the man who he felt took his life away from him.

Malik sat outside of Montario's house patiently waiting on a way to get in the house. Malik was camped out and was totally incognito. Montario's wife pulled in the driveway and let up the garage door. At the same time, she was letting the garage door up her children were opening the front door of the house. Malik stayed still until he seen an opportunity for him to slip into the garage without being seen. Once he slipped in the garage he ducked off and waited for his next move.

Montario and his family were in the house doing what they did every day. His wife was cooking, the kids were doing homework, and he was on his computer doing business. After snitching on Malik, Montario got out the game. He used the money he made with Malik to fund the two different businesses he owned. He was doing well for himself and turned into the family man his wife always prayed for him to be. Usually by the time dinner was done everyone would be done with what they were doing, then they would sit at the table and eat as a family. They had a dining room table big enough to seat all five of them plus a few guests.

Montario and his wife were doing their own thing, so they didn't notice that every time one of their children went into the garage they never returned. The kids were always in and out the garage because that's where all the bottled waters and soft drinks were stored. Malik snatched up every one of Montario's children as they came into the garage. He found rope to tie them with and found tape to tape their mouths shut. He wanted to kill the children right then and there but decided to wait.

It was time for dinner before Montario and his wife recognized that their children weren't running around the house making noise. After his wife called the kid's names multiple times and no one said anything Montario went to the back of the house to get his children. He thought that maybe the TV volumes were too high for his kids to hear their names being called. As he went to the back Malik slipped in the house and snatched up Montario's wife, he tied her up quickly. Montario came back to the front of the house with the surprise of a lifetime looking him right in his eyes.

"So, you repay the nigga that took you from nothing to something by testifying on him and getting him fifty years in prison," asked Malik as he stared into Montario's eyes?

"My wife told me it was the best thing for me to do, so I did it," said Montario as he looked at his wife trying to get the blame off him.

"You're a fucking pussy. And I would let you go Tamika, but you really looked me in my eyes when I got sentenced and told me I got what I deserved. And Montario you're just a pussy to put the blame on your bitch," said Malik as he hit Montario in the mouth knocking him straight to the floor.

After Malik knocked him out, he tied him up and taped his mouth closed. He went and got all the children out the garage after that. Malik got heavy duty trash bags out of Montario's kitchen. He placed each one of Montario's kids in separate bags and tied the bags up to suffocate them to death. This made Montario and Tamika try to break loose, but there was nothing they could do. The silent tears that rolled down their faces was the only way they could show the pain they were going through.

"Both of you punk ass bitches thought it was okay to take me away from my family, but now you want to cry like bitches. After all I did for you two bitches and these three bastards. You little bastards die slow and I want both of you bitches to watch them die slowly before I kill you motherfuckers too," said Malik.

Malik grabbed Montario's phone off the table and started to touch the screen navigating to his purpose of picking up the phone. He put it on Spades Plus and played a game of spades before putting the phone down, by this time the kids were dead. He then picked up Montario's wife and pulled her pants down enough for him to fuck her from the back as hard as he could right in Montario's face. Malik fucked her hard in the ass until there was blood pouring out her asshole. He then got up with a smile on his face as he walked towards Montario. Just before he made it to Montario he turned around and went back to the garage.

He returned with a weed eater and started it up in the living room. Once it was on, he put his finger on the throttle and began to let it chop at Montario's face. After making Montario suffer by weed eating his whole-body Malik stopped and let him feel the pain. Malik played another game of spades on Montario's phone before he cut his throat with the weed eater. Malik sat Indian style on the floor as he watched Montario die. Once Montario was dead Malik tied up Montario's wife tighter and told her he was going to let her live.

"You looked me in my eyes and told me I got what I deserved when I was taken away from my family now, I'm telling you the same thing. I took your family away from you now bitch and I hope it feels good to you," said Malik as he spit in her face before leaving.

CHAPTER 19

Lil Drama was knee deep in Lilian's pussy when Malik entered the bedroom unnoticed.

"Fuck me baby, fuck me and take all my misery away," said Lilian as Lil Drama laid on top of her humping her like a rabbit.

"You better say this pussy mine you pretty bitch," demanded Lil Drama.

"It's yours baby, just fuck me," replied Lilian.

"Where do you want this nut at," asked Lil Drama?

"Put it in my mouth right now. I want to suck it until you come in my mouth," said Lilian.

Right when Lil Drama was about to put his dick in Lilian's mouth, Malik hit them both with a high voltage stun gun. Then he tied up Lil Drama and waited for them both to be fully aware again. Lilian woke up first and Malik punched her in the stomach so hard that she lost her wind. Malik was surprised that she was in his house fucking one of his old friends. He was determined to make her feel the pain though.

"So, you fucking this punk ass nigga, huh," asked Malik as he put tape on Lil Drama's mouth?

"Malik I'm sorry, please don't do this. What is wrong with you," asked Lilian?

"There is nothing left to say. Bitch you, him, and all the kids will be dead before I leave this house. After all we than did and the respect I had for you, you going to fuck somebody I know," said Malik.

As he talked Lil Drama was beginning to gain consciousness again.

"You said you wanted this nigga dick in your mouth so go suck his dick bitch while I watch," said

Malik as he smacked her in the back of the head because she didn't move fast enough.

Lilian refused, but once Malik started to poke her with thumb tacks, she couldn't take the pain, so she got down and started giving Lil Drama head. Malik let her have her way giving him head for a few minutes then he told her to stop. While Lil Drama was still on rock hard Malik pulled out a razor knife and made Lilian sliced his dick. He made her start at his pee hole and slice all the way down to his balls even cutting his nut sack opened as well. Lilian dreaded doing it, but Malik made it clear he would kill one of their children if she didn't and she knew he was serious. Lil Drama moved around on the floor in pain as blood squirted from his penis and nut sack.

"I love this shit. I love when somebody think they can get over on me because I come back like a thief in the night every time. You slut ass bitch I can't believe you. There is no telling who else you been fucking out here," said Malik before he started singing a song.

That's when he tied Lilian up and taped her mouth shut. He went into his children rooms and tied them up one by one. His children were overwhelmed with joy when they saw their father, but he didn't have any emotion towards them. After he had everyone in one room, he made up a game to play which would determine who died first. The whole time they played the game Malik was stabbing Lil Drama's already dead body.

As Malik was stabbing Lil Drama the doorbell to the house rang. Malik was just going to let whoever it was stand outside until they left. Then he looked at the camera monitors and seen it was his mother. At that moment his heart dropped, and he ran to the door. He was going to play it off like he was there alone so she wouldn't know what was going on at first. After a few seconds of thinking about it he changed his mind.

Malik opened the door and hit his mother so hard in the face that she fell to the ground. The punch he gave her came from nowhere. He pulled her in the house and tied her up with everybody else in the house. When his mother regained her consciousness, she was in the room with Lilian and her grandchildren tied up. Malik then began to talk and express his feelings.

"Just so that both of you will know, I'm the one who killed my father Sharp, I did it and I'm proud of it," said Malik as Lilian looked at him with a surprised look on her face.

"Yeah, bitch Sharp was my father, so you fucked father and son just like you like to fuck friend's nasty ass bitch," said Malik again as he looked Lilian in her face before spitting in her face.

"Then my mother of all people never told me who my father was, and you know what I went through as a child not knowing. I made a vowel to kill you Tammy the night you told me who my father was you dirty bitch," said Malik.

Malik stood there telling stories about all the emotional pain he had went through not knowing his father all his life. He told his mother that all she had to do was say something. He told her he didn't give a fuck about Sharp saying he would kill them and told her he felt that was only an excuse for her to use. He informed her that it was too late for her to take it back and she had to suffer the consequences. Malik assured her that it wasn't him doing what he was doing, instead it was her actions. Malik was preparing to torture everyone in the room until Tammy broke loose.

Tammy didn't want to expose her gift in front of Lilian and the kids because she knew she would have to kill them if she exposed it in front of them. She just acted like she broke loose and after breaking loose she charged at Malik. She punched him so hard in his side that she broke more than one of his ribs. That's when Malik thought about what the spirits told him about his mother being the primary holder of the gift, they both had. He knew that meant she had more power than him, so he knew he had to think fast.

Malik jumped back to his feet and ran out the house so fast that you wouldn't have been able to clock his speed with a radar gun. That's when his mother knew that she was going to have to kill her son whenever she was to find him. Malik had a gift, but he couldn't control it, so it made him a dangerous man. Their gift was something you had to gradually come into connection with through meditation. With all the hatred Malik had in his heart she knew the only way to tame her son was through her killing him. The look in her eyes when Malik jumped to his feet and ran off said death. If only Lilian and the kids weren't there, she would have chased him down and killed him then.

"Malik must die," is what the spirit said to Tammy as she watched her son vanish into thin air.

She knew she was in for a battle only because Malik was reckless, but she hoped since she was the dominant possessor of the gift that she would overcome him in the long run. This was now a superhuman battle. The wise one was the one who would survive the battle because neither of them could totally win the battle.

THE END

Eric Williams

Contact me for book signings, speaking engagements, or just some uplifting words at:

ericw8403@gmail.com

CPSIA information can be obtained
at www.ICGtesting.com
Printed in the USA
LVHW091606061120
670968LV00002B/213